'She forgot the map,' grinne<
rather tatty piece of paper, wł
souvenir,' he said, 'of your h<
    'I think I would like rathei
paper,' I said.

    'How about this?' and bejure i cuuiu repiy ne nuu
wrapped his arm around my shoulders and kissed me
lightly on the lips.

Flora McGowan is the author of the *Carrie and Keith
Mysteries.* These stories combine a mix of mystery
with the mystical and supernatural, often with an
historical element as well as a touch of humour.
Flora was born in Dorset and has spent much of her
life there, setting many of her stories in this locale.
She enjoys travelling, taking inspiration from the
places she visits.
You can catch up with Flora via Goodreads, her
blog, Facebook or Instagram where she posts
photographs of many of the places that feature in
her stories, as well as associated items such as
Victorian mourning cloaks and the wedding dress
that featured in her debut novel.

Also available by Flora McGowan:

Carrie and Keith Mysteries:
Material Witness
Thirteen in the Medina

Carrie and Keith Short Stories:
Seasonal Shorts
The Way to Nowhere (digital short story)
All at Sea (digital short story)
The Case of the Haunted Wig (digital short story)
A Match Made in Heaven (digital short story)

Short Story Collections (as contributor):
The Phantom Games
Fate's Call
Not Just Soldiers: Aid For Ukraine
The West Country Collection
The Ultimate Short Story Collection
The Little Shop of Murders

This book is dedicated to my sister, Diana – I hope you like it

Also, with grateful thanks to my sister, Christina, and my niece, Briony, with grateful thanks for their help, suggestions and most of all patience

Cover design by vcbookcovers.com

Images from Shutterstock

Playing with Fire

Flora McGowan

Prologue One:

Summer 2011

The house was located in the midst of Lazio in central Italy, a region containing not only the country's capital, Rome, with its ancient Forum, the Coliseum, and the more recent Baroque additions of the Trevi Fountain and the Spanish Steps, but also the Vatican, the spiritual and physical heart of the Roman Catholic Church; while on the coast sits Ostia with its ancient port. The Tyrrhenian sea, with Tuscany and Umbria to the north, comprise its borders, with Campania to the south.

It was an imposing villa, surrounded by well-maintained gardens and secure high walls. Nevertheless, the man scaled the walls with ease and gained entry into the house in a similarly carefree manner. He had been supplied with a detailed floor plan and once inside quickly moved to his room of choice where he carefully consulted his list of instructions; it would not do to purloin the wrong

1

item.

The cabinet was locked, of course, but that posed no problems; he dealt with it as effortlessly as he had the rest of the household security devices. It contained a fine array of small statuary from the classical Roman period; not high-quality copies or tourist mementoes but genuine antique treasures sculpted a couple of millennia ago.

He soon spied the figure he had been despatched to collect located towards the back on the middle shelf; it fitted snugly into his large hand and he noted with a sudden feeling of pleasure the cool, smooth surface of the polished marble. He gazed admiringly into the finely crafted features of the face, the curves of the beard, the hair swept back from the wide forehead, the eyes seeming to portray the pride of an artisan as he endeavoured to ply his skill; the left arm raised in movement, capturing the moment of industry.

He swiftly secreted the statue in a small velvet bag and thrust it deep into the secure inner pocket of his jacket; then after casting one last yearning glance over the rest of the objects on display he quietly closed the cabinet doors and turned his back on all the finely wrought and extremely expensive sculptures that had the ability to tempt him to take another piece that was not on his list, just one tiny piece to keep for his own personal enjoyment; it was a shame he could not do that; the outcome would be unthinkable.

With a self-satisfied smile he rubbed his hands with glee. Job done.

Prologue Two

And so, here I was in Sicily.

With the outbreak of the Arab Spring my holiday plans had been thrown into disarray, and I had thought that as an alternative Sicily might be a good, *safe*, destination.

I should have thought harder, for longer.

I should have considered the Mafia, and other small time crooks.

I should have factored in the cranks that you encounter on organised tours.

And I should have taken into account the locals that you meet, who turn your life, not to mention your head and your heart, upside down.

Chapter One

Strangers on a Plane

September 2011

I was in Taormina when I first saw him.

Vanessa had disappeared into a shop. Again. She was looking for something, or so she claimed, but refused to divulge what. Each time she had ventured into the bowels of a store she had given a suggestive wink with an accompanying grin as if to imply that it was a huge secret, her lips were sealed and wild horses wouldn't drag any further information from her. Joan and I were firmly instructed to remain outside. I was beginning to regret agreeing to join them for our free time in the town.

When we had earlier disembarked from the bus Vanessa had approached me saying, 'Hello, you're on your own as well, aren't you? Come and join Joan and me.' She had indicated the smaller, dark haired woman who hovered uncertainly behind her. 'I'm Vanessa by the way.' She appeared confident and outgoing, and I thought, perhaps that was what I needed in a strange town in a foreign country, to team up with someone who seemed to know what they were doing, and so I had agreed. However, like many snap decisions that seemed like a good idea at the time, I was now having grave doubts.

It was a little unusual to start a touring holiday with free time but it is never too early to begin souvenir shopping, especially when not only do I desire to purchase a little memento (or two) for myself but also gifts for my sister and nephew, not forgetting the multitude of postcards I needed to send to family and friends.

Mary, our tour manager, had informed us there was an impressive nativity scene that was worth seeing, which was displayed in a church at the end of the long main street; it seemed it was on view all year round. She had also advised us to have some lunch before the group met up again prior to our visit to the nearby Greek amphitheatre. At the rate Vanessa was going we would not have time for both. I gritted my teeth and bit back any words of censure I might have been thinking; the first day of a holiday is not the time to make enemies.

Vanessa, having first agreed that perusing the shops was a good idea, (here Joan had nodded in acquiescence), and yes, she would like to see the nativity, (and again Joan had nodded), kept darting off into various shops saying to us, 'Just wait here a minute' whilst she disappeared, sometimes for quite a period of time and I was getting a little frustrated

6

with her behaviour. In the end I decided to leave Joan patiently waiting, and wandered further along the high street, looking in the windows to browse the range of tourist souvenirs on offer.

There was the usual mix of tea towels, miniature, and not so miniature statues of the Greek gods in various poses, various items with the three-legged symbol of Sicily that reminded me of the Isle of Man emblem, and bottles of obligatory alcohol although some of these latter items I shuddered to think any sane person would purchase. These bottles (and not just wine bottles, there were also condiment sets and diverse items such as picture frames) were "decorated" with lumps of rock – lava - it was claimed, from Mount Etna, however these pieces were created in such a fashion as to appear as if the glass was encrusted with pustules of some sort of contagious vitreous pox.

I looked at my watch to judge the time; we still had to eat and had yet to find the nativity scene and half our free time had already been eaten away, mostly by hanging around waiting for Vanessa to do whatever it was she was doing. I peered up the street to gauge how much further it might continue and whether I could spot any buildings as likely candidates for our destination. We had already entered the local library in error thinking that it looked a suitable church-like building to house a nativity. As far as I could tell we were near the end of the town; we were running out of possible locations for the diorama.

And that was when I had spied the man. He also

7

appeared to be searching for someone, or something.

Even after having to rethink my holiday plans there had been problems.

On arriving at Gatwick airport I had managed to check myself in and chosen an aisle seat then proceeded to do likewise with my luggage; however, the conveyer belt had broken and so all suitcases had had to be stacked one on top of the other on trolleys, before being manually transported across the airport. I gazed wistfully at my (new) case as I walked away, wondering if I would ever see it again.

After easing my way through the endless queues of security, I had lingered briefly in the duty free. I used to sample the expensive perfume testers until I was left one holiday enduring a flight with a throbbing headache. Therefore, I sat for the intervening time – one hour, two hours, then three hours – my heart sinking as the announcement came that the flight was delayed, and read my book. Eventually, the gate opened and I joined the throng. More security.

And then there was the wait before boarding. Ten minutes, twenty minutes. Those requiring assistance were allowed to enter the plane, those with small children, those with special passes, then those with seats at the back, in the middle (me), the remaining passengers.

There was a slight hold up as a couple were blocking the aisle while they tipped out the contents from their bag onto a seat searching for books, reading glasses, magazines; they edged to one side to allow me to squeeze past. I looked down at the seat they had covered with their belongings and hesitantly informed them, 'That's my seat.'

Reluctantly, they had scooped their stuff up and onto the centre seat allowing me to sit down. Those passengers queuing patiently behind me were then able to pass and find their own places. Eventually everyone was settled.

I don't particularly like flying, but it is the quickest way to travel. This plane was on the smallish side, three seats each side of a central aisle. With dismay I realised it had no entertainment other than the inflight magazine (stained), the safety card (well thumbed) and the brochure of inflight goods for sale (both stained and well thumbed). There was not a single TV screen offering any sort of visual distraction and no radio.

Being prone to travel sickness as a child I did not want to read my book, the print being a little on the small side, besides at this rate, after the time spent reading in the departure area, I would finish it before I even landed in Sicily. It would have to be the inflight magazine until the food arrived, it now being 8pm and I had not eaten since a light snack at midday.

It had been dark when we landed in Catania, but pleasantly warm and dry. Customs was uneventful, however, my case was one of the last to arrive on the revolving conveyer belt, (the downside of arriving early at the airport to ensure I did not miss the plane, as the suitcase is then likely to be one of the first to be loaded into the hold), and I was beginning to panic. Other passengers had collected their luggage and were congregating in an ever-increasing mass in the corner. I did not want to be last. I did not want my brand new case to be lost or damaged on its first excursion. Any minute now, I thought, our group leader, Mary, who had introduced herself in the departure area, would gather everyone together and leave for the hotel and I would be left alone, still waiting for my case at the carousel. I envisaged it still stacked on the trolley awaiting transit back at Gatwick.

I glanced around at those few remaining stragglers awaiting their bags like me – were any of them part of our group?

Eventually my case appeared, miraculously intact and I hurried over to join the throng.

Mary did another head count and, satisfied, thrust her umbrella in the air - tour leaders always have umbrellas; it is not an indication of the likely weather to be encountered, thankfully, although we did encounter stormy times, but how tour guides indicate their presence and gather in their minions – and led us outside to the waiting coach.

The drive to the hotel was relatively short and uneventful. I tried to look out the windows but somehow the drive from the airport through the surrounding countryside was uninspiring; perhaps because it was late at night and I was feeling somewhat jaded after the long wait and then the flight.

On arrival at the hotel we had been herded into the dining room for a late night snack of sandwiches and coffee. After our "snackpot" on the plane I was more than ready for food, as were my fellow travellers. They converged on the tables with plates at the ready, men shovelling sandwiches onto them, others like myself a little more wary, trying to decipher the handwritten labels attached to toothpicks stuck into the pinnacle of each pile. Unfortunately, these seemed to be written in some sort of secret code. I kept my eye on a lady to my left who was engaging in the age old method of sandwich discovery, in that she would lift a corner of the bread and mutter 'cheese' or 'fish paste' before moving on to the next platter. She did not necessarily take the sandwich that she had fingered.

She caught me watching, and leaning towards me smiled and said, 'The labels aren't much help, are they? I think these are ham and tomato, and those over there,' she nodded to her right, 'are egg.' She smiled at me alarmingly, revealing large discoloured uneven teeth. 'I'm Dottie.' She added.

I thought, 'Perhaps you are,' then realising she was introducing herself and not giving her mental state, replied, 'Carrie.'

'Have you travelled with this company before?' she asked as we made our way with laden plates to one of the tables arranged down the left-hand side of the room. Once seated she continued to touch everything, hand around cups, poke her nose into pots to discover if they contained tea or coffee, in an effort to be helpful. As with the food I quickly selected my own cup and saucer making sure it had not been manhandled first.

Already seated at the table was a very upright, austere looking elderly lady, with straight iron-grey hair cut in an extremely short back and sides style. Dottie introduced both herself and me, to which this lady replied in very plummy tones, 'Millie.'

'I say,' Millie continued, 'it's awfully good of them to feed us like this isn't it? I mean that food on the plane wasn't very nice was it? Or did you like it? I didn't; thought it was ghastly. Would you like some more tea?' She caught the attention of a passing waiter.

Well, I thought, I need not have worried about holidaying alone. I seemed to have made two new friends already.

By the time I had finishing eating the late supper and located my room on the first floor my case was already waiting for me outside the door. I duly inserted the plastic key into the slot and held my breath that it worked. The green light duly winked at me and I pushed the door open. Inside it was pitch dark. I groped around for light switches but could elicit no illumination. By means of feeling on the wall behind the door I located what I took to be the holder for the electric card, however no card was in evidence. A cursory glance around the room revealed little in what illumination entered from the hallway.

There was no one else around to ask; either those on my corridor had retired already or were still downstairs eating. There was nothing for it but to admit defeat and go and ask at the check-in desk for assistance.

As I went down the stairs to reception I could see a man I thought I recognised as being a member of our party talking to the man at the desk. As I moved closer I thought he looked like the man who had been seated next to me on the plane, who along with the woman had been emptying the contents of their bag onto my seat. Mostly during the flight I had only side glimpses of his profile. For a tourist who had just arrived an hour or two earlier he seemed remarkably chatty with the locals. They fell silent as I approached and both turned towards me, though not, I thought, particularly hospitably.

'There are no lights in my room,' I began.

The man turned to me and confirmed my suspicions that he was one of us by saying, 'Mary told us that the key controls the electrics.' He gesticulated with his plastic room "key," attached to which was a chunky handle. 'Put this into the slot behind the door.'

'I thought she said a card, not a key,' I said, refusing to feel stupid on my first night of my holidays.

I thanked the man, after all he was part of our group and I did not want to fall out with anyone so early in the trip, and returned to my room.

Back in my room with the key fob duly inserted

into the slot and lo! there was light. Umm, I almost preferred the room when it had been submerged in darkness. It was a good-sized room but sparsely furnished; bleak and cheerless. A peek through the blind elicited no view but the sounds from the kitchens drifted up as the staff cleared away the remains of our late night supper. As I had previously commented to a fellow traveller, the single person always gets the worst rooms but pays the highest price: the smallest room tucked away in the attic, the room with the sea view blocked by trees, the room by the lifts with people constantly coming and going, the sounds and the smells from the kitchens.

I had prepared for bed feeling more than a little despondent than earlier in the day when I had been looking forward to my holiday; the room was not quite what I had hoped for, no view to speak of and at present I was loath to open the window for fresh air due to the closeness of the kitchens. However, I appeared to have made two friends at least; so what if they were both about the same age as my gran, that did not mean they did not know how to enjoy themselves (though I would have to watch some of Dottie's habits, such as handling everything and tasting the food).

Sitting up in bed I turned over in my mind the other possible places I could have taken for a vacation. I hoped I had not made a mistake in coming here; I hoped I was about to enjoy this holiday.

*

After breakfast, an above average fare with a selection of fresh fruit and yogurt, cereal, bread and pastries, and the usual attempt by continental hotels of the cooked English breakfast, fatty streaky bacon in a warming dish next to congealed scrambled egg in another warming dish (if only some people were not so lazy and could remember to lower the lid of the dish, food might actually then keep warm), with fruit juice and tea or coffee, we ambled out to take our seats in the bus for our visit to Taormina, a town on the coast a little to the north of Sicily, situated atop a hill.

Despite the tour company being one of those who allocate seats and enforce rotation on a coach in an attempt, they claim, to promote fairness and decrease time in decision making as to where to sit, due to a mix up in the seating plan Mary said I could sit on the back seat, that being officially vacant.

However, when I approached I found a man, who introduced himself as Richard, ensconced in the middle of the back seat, his long, thin legs stretched out before him and various bags bundled to right and left. With what presumably he thought was a sexy leer he asked if I was joining him and I carefully squeezed into the seat to his right. I was arranging my own bag, containing hat, camera etc, when a commotion broke out.

'There's someone sitting in my seat! I counted very carefully from the front and I am supposed to be sitting in row nine.'

I thought I recognised the plummy vowels and

glanced up. Millie, looking a bit distraught, was standing in the aisle.

'There's someone sitting in my seat,' she wailed again. If there was, no guilty party moved or offered to do so. 'Mind if I sit on the back seat with you?' She eased herself past Richard's bags to the seat on his left. 'I say, there's no point in having a seating plan if people aren't going to stick to it!'

'I think we have more room on the back seat,' I said by way of consolation.

'It's been a while since I have had two ladies on the back seat,' added Richard with another leer, and looking at his sparse figure I thought, yes that's probably true.

Millie snapped her mouth shut as if she could not bring herself to comment on this innuendo. She gazed out the window with the air of someone who has never in her whole life before sat on a back seat.

Chapter Two

A Funny Thing Happened on the Way to the Amphitheatre

I am not sure what first made me stop and stare at the man; it might have been his curly hair; not the tight curls of an Afro perm but more the soft fat curls like those clustered atop of Shirley Temple's head; only his curls were grey being a shade lighter than the iron grey of Millie's hair. And when he turned his head, as he gazed around as if searching for someone, I noticed that his skin, although tanned similarly to the other native Sicilians compared to my pale English complexion, was smooth and wrinkle-free, except for the frown that marred his brow. With that colour hair I expected to see a more mature person, but then I doubted an older man would have retained his curly locks but more likely to have clipped them closer to his skull. Added to the comparatively youthful face was a finely proportioned torso that stood astride a bicycle as he stopped, eyes searching up and down the main street. I guessed he was aged about thirty, although I am usually no good at guessing people's ages; however, he was a lot younger when viewed from the front than a view from behind would have supposed.

It was at this point that Vanessa and Joan reappeared both eating ice-cream, and when I looked around again the man was gone. I felt a sudden impulse to chide my companions that they might ruin their appetite for lunch but bit my tongue instead; it was too early in the day to annoy people although Vanessa seemed to be making a good job of that. I mentally counted to five by which time they had drawn level, and I resumed my trek in search of the tiny church with what we were informed was a huge nativity; I hoped it was worth all this effort.

We duly found the object of our quest and stood for a few moments admiring the extensive miniature village scene, the centre piece of which was the manger holding the baby Jesus, while all around the tiny villagers continued with their everyday life.

Then we quickly retraced our steps back down the street, this time in search of a café or restaurant suitable for a spot of lunch. Again, Vanessa took the lead deciding she had found an eatery that fulfilled our requirements; not too pricey and with tables set up outside so that we could sit in the sun. She immediately ordered a glass of white wine from a passing waiter even before Joan and I had had a chance to look at the menu and agree with her choice.

Both Joan and I declined to drink alcohol at lunchtime; I rarely drink alcohol midday, even on holiday, as I prefer to keep my alcohol rations for the evening whilst keeping a sensible level of hydration during the day when under a hot sun. Joan stated she was teetotal; I think that was the only comment she offered throughout the meal. Mostly Vanessa talked about herself, her house, her work, her other holidays, while I concentrated on eating the cannelloni I had chosen. Joan had ordered something with chicken while Vanessa had selected a veal dish that she picked at occasionally, eating with only a fork after cutting everything into bite sized pieces, her other hand she alternatively waved around to illustrate as she spoke, or used to pick up her wine glass.

I consulted my watch with concern when she ordered a second white wine; we did not have to time to sit and lazily drink in the sun; we needed to think about the meeting time and place. Again, I regretted agreeing to join up with Vanessa and Joan; idly I wondered what Dottie and Millie were up to.

Somehow, we made it to the meeting point on time by the skin of our teeth and, miraculously we were not last. It is always a disaster on a holiday to be the last person to turn up for an excursion or a meeting on the first day – you are then forever marked as a poor timekeeper, despite the fact that it might be a one-off event or that there may have been an extremely good reason for your tardiness. Excuses are heard with disdain and the embarrassment lingers.

The Greek amphitheatre was a spectacular experience with which to start the tour of the island (discounting our ramble through the town of Taormina). With Mount Etna looming in the background (actually Mount Etna looms over just about everything) and the sparkling waters of the Mediterranean Sea visible to one side and the clear blue sky above, it was perfect.

I tried to mingle in with the rest of our group (ie, lose Joan and more importantly Vanessa but they followed me around doggedly) as Mary led us in through the theatre entrance, around the stage area to the orchestra pit, and I listened to her explanations, while all the time my mind was on being able to clamber up the stairs between the rows of stone seats to experience the view. Then we moved up the next tier and the extent of the panorama began to unfold. Eventually the mini lecture was over and the group was set free to wander. Relieved, I legged it as fast as I could up the nearest flight of stone steps.

As expected the view was magnificent, stretching for what seemed like miles. I took a few photos with my camera and then started to walk along the periphery behind the back row, stopping in the middle to take some more shots.

I was just lowering my camera when Vanessa

appeared at my side, Joan a couple of steps behind her.

'I can't seem to get my camera to work,' Vanessa complained. 'Are you any good with these things?' She held the offending item out towards me. I dutifully took it, switched it on and peered at the square viewing pane. There were lots of little squiggles and icons and something flashing in red.

'I'm not sure,' I began hesitantly, passing the camera back, 'but I think maybe your battery needs recharging.'

Vanessa took the camera back with a grunt of dissatisfaction and was about to say something else when a dark shadow passed over us. I looked up in dismay thinking that sudden clouds were going to ruin my enjoyment of this visit only to find a rather obese gentleman in a somewhat tight t-shirt hovering with a camera in his hand that he was in the process of trying to pass to me.

'Pleeze, you take photo?' he asked, grinning and gesturing at himself and his equally portly friend.

I did not think I could refuse; after all he had said, 'Pleeze.' He must have thought I was handing Vanessa's camera back after having taken a picture for her. Therefore, I accepted the camera and by pointing and fiddling ascertained which button to press to take the picture and which worked the telephoto lever, and then stepped back a little while the two men struck up suitably dramatic poses on the back row of seats. Then they changed positions so they stood against a background of the stone seating areas sweeping downwards to the auditorium with Etna behind them blowing little white puffs into the air on their right and the blue sea to the left.

I took a couple of photos of the men then they persuaded Vanessa (who had not needed that much persuasion) and Joan to join them for a group shot, and I handed the camera back.

As I did so I just happened to glance up and see the top of a head covered in grey curls disappear out an exit side door in a squarish tower leading to a flight of stairs. I was momentarily distracted while the tubby man was enquiring whether we would like him to reciprocate and take photos of us. Quick as a flash Vanessa impressed her camera on him and I left her trying to explain that she was not sure why it was not working and hurried over towards the side exit. As Vanessa and the stranger stood in a huddle peering at the camera I had the fleeting impression that something else had changed hands as well as the camera.

It was dark inside the tower where the stone steps led back down to the ground floor level. I had to go carefully so as not to miss my footing on the worn, irregular staircase thus when I emerged once more into the sunlight and gazed around there was no grey-haired head to be seen. A little despondently I moved towards the exit.

I was not sure why I was curious about the man; and why I should be surprised to see him in the amphitheatre; perhaps he was on holiday just like us and having done a little shopping in town this morning, as our group had done, he had now viewed the main attraction in the area, the Greek theatre. It was as simple as that, there was no mystery. However, that did not stop me wondering as to who he might be.

We had one more port of call before heading back to the hotel to freshen up before dinner, a trip to the Alcantara Gorge, an area of natural beauty. Mary explained, as we drove up in the coach, that in ancient times Etna had erupted causing lava to flow into the area, which the river had subsequently eroded away creating the high walls of the canyon. She further added that there were two stretches of the river that we could investigate: there was an upper stream with a scenic walk bordered by flowering shrubs, or we could go down in a lift to a wider river expanse where we might see canoeists practising their craft; or if we walked quickly, we might have time to explore both sections.

On holiday I am definitely a person who wants to see and do most things that are on offer so deciding that the walk along the upper section would take the most time I opted to do that first. I alighted the bus promptly and made my way towards the toilets so that I was prepared for a brisk walk. Outside the toilet block, after Mary had paid the necessary entrance fee, she was handing out tickets in the form of little coloured bracelets that indicated we had paid to be able to see both upper and lower sections. I had collected mine and was about to set off when Vanessa called me back:

'Wait for me,' she implored, 'I just need to nip in the loo.'

I looked at my watch and waited. Why was it, I thought, that Vanessa had been hanging around outside chatting to Joan and Dottie, and as soon as everyone else was ready she decided she needed to use the toilet? Why didn't she go in there earlier? I thought a little irritatedly. When Vanessa finally re-appeared we were the only three people left in the entrance area; most had gone down in the lift to the river at the lower level. I set off purposefully along the path marking the course along the banks of the upper stream leaving Vanessa to break into a little run to catch up, with Joan trotting along behind her.

After about ten minutes of striding alongside the river bank flanked by tall grasses and bushy shrubs Vanessa declared she had had enough and was turning back. I heaved a sigh of relief and continued on my way. Unfortunately, as I had failed to follow her lead Vanessa continued to traipse along behind me, muttering cajolingly every few minutes, 'Let's go down to the bottom stream now, we've seen enough here!'

Once or twice I answered, 'Just a bit further' and sometimes I ignored her, hoping she might just go away and leave me in peace. After another ten minutes we encountered two couples from our group, Tom and Angela, and Paul and Christine, coming back along the path.

'Did you make it to the end of the trail?' I asked them. 'Is it far?'

'Just a bit further,' replied Paul. 'There's a large clump of cactus by the side of the path; that seems to be about as far as it goes.'

I thanked them and increased my pace a little now that the end was in sight. The stream had gradually widened as we had walked along its banks, with small boulders in the water creating little waterfalls. Now, nearing the end of the trail the boulders obstructing the flow were getting larger and spray rose in the air like a fine mist all around me. I spied the cactus just as the path ended at a large rocky outcrop; the river widened and disappeared into the distance. I took a few photos, then consulted my watch; there was still plenty of time to go to the lower level, and retraced my steps back towards the lift.

Vanessa was still stomping slowly up the path, Joan in her wake but when I appeared they turned and accompanied me back along the stony track. I made another mental note that if this illustrated their degree of interest in the countryside then tomorrow I would seek some more interesting and interested companions for the proposed trek up Mount Etna.

Back at the entrance area I considered the lift suspiciously; it looked a little antiquated. There were supposed to be steps going down but they were roped off and appeared to be closed to the public, therefore we had no alternative but to trust in the ancient mechanism. However, as Joan pointed out, everyone else appeared to have safely gone down –

no-one was up here! Thus I breathed deeply and entered the tiny dark cubical.

I do not like lifts. It is not just the confined space, being shut in a small, dark area but also the movement, be it up or down, disconcerts me. I have read that this may be due to motion sensors in the ear, and the unpleasant sensation can be eased a little if you stand to one side and tilt your head. Vanessa, of course, was taking charge of the control panel although there did not seem to be much choice; the lift only went down to the lower ground level and back up again. However, Vanessa was suddenly in an impish mood and announced;

'I wonder what this button does?' and moved as if to press an oddly marked button to one side.

'Don't!' I cried loudly, slapping her hand quickly away from the button. She looked at me in sudden alarm and the thought occurred to me that perhaps not many people had ever said that to her before. A little sheepishly she pressed the correct button and down we descended.

When the doors opened I allowed the others to leave the confines of the cubical first while I breathed deeply, relieved that we had made it safely to our destination before I followed them out, leaving a respectful distance between us.

The lower level of the gorge was spectacular and very different to the river we had walked beside earlier. Here massive cliffs arose both sides of a wide but shallow stream. Whilst the water stretched further it was evident that it soon deepened dramatically hence people were clustered in the shallows. Children shrieked and paddled in the waters while their parents looked on indulgently. I trudged across the shingle banks to where I spied Millie and Dottie who asked about the walk along the upper level. I described my hike and then we decided to emulate the younger element and removed our sandals for a more sedate paddle.

The water was refreshingly cool and revived my hot, tired feet. We moved slowly about in the water so as not to produce too much splash. I decided that I had made the correct decision in viewing the upper level first, which took the most time as there was little to see and do here except paddle. All too soon it was time to replace our footwear and depart.

I managed to avoid Vanessa and Joan, and made the return journey up in the lift with Dottie and Millie. It was only possible to squeeze a handful of people into the tiny cubical at one time. We judged it just right, before the mass exodus, and hence we made a relatively comfortable ascent and then headed for the shop where after a quick perusal I bought a postcard of the gorge to send to my friend, Pat, and a tea towel for my sister, Harriet. While I waited to board the bus I found my eyes searching the car park in vain; but there was no sign of any grey curly haired men with bicycles.

During the ride back to our hotel Mary briefly outlined the arrangements for our trip to Mount Etna scheduled for tomorrow. The coach would deposit us at the car park at the base of the volcano, where there are a few shops and a café. Anyone wishing to do so could take the cable car up to the next level where there was another small café with a shopping area. There we could walk a little further to see the views over the surrounding countryside. From this level it was possible to ride in jeeps to the summit of the volcano; however, unfortunately we would not have time to do this, which seemed a little curious as we had nothing else planned on the itinerary for the rest of the day.

The weather forecast was for another fine day but Mary advised sensible shoes and perhaps a cardi or sweater as it might be breezy. She recommended we think about whether we wanted to make the climb and she would assess the numbers wishing to do so tomorrow and then decide on the amount of time we would we permitted to remain on the slopes; if too few people wished to experience the cable cars – and here it sounded as if she hoped no-one would – we would make only a brief visit and return for free time in the hotel, perhaps, she suggested, for a swim in the pool?

I listened to this with a sinking heart. It sounded as if Mary had no interest in visiting the volcano. This is one of the downsides of having an English tour manager on holiday; if a travel company employs a native of that country to lead the group, and not just as guides at various sites I have always found them superior to a non-resident, being knowledgeable about their country and usually extremely proud and keen to show it off – that is, after all, the main reason why they chose that line of work, other than for employment.

If we had had a native Sicilian tour leader he would have been extolling the features of the visit, the geology, the history of eruptions, whilst urging us to make the ascent, to make time for the jeep ride, while all Mary could say was to suggest sensible shoes.

At the thought of a native Sicilian my eyes strayed out the window as if in search of a man riding a bicycle. But what if he was not Sicilian or even Italian? If he was, as I had surmised, a tourist like myself then he could be from any country; why he could even be British like myself! And with that disquieting thought I slumped back in my seat in dismay.

I thought perhaps I might have had too much to drink, or maybe the wine at dinner was stronger than I was used to, causing some sort of auditory hallucination, but I was sure that Dottie had said something about Arthur sleeping at the base of Mount Etna. Then I thought possibly she had a friend who had emigrated to Sicily and lived somewhere in the area. I hesitantly sipped my wine and then looked around in the sudden silence. Unless we were suffering from group auditory hallucinations she must have said something odd for everyone to be staring at her. Flustered, she hemmed and hawed a bit, picked up her drink then replaced it on the coffee table untasted.

'Well, I meant to say,' she began but could think of nothing to add.

It was, somewhat surprisingly, Patrick, the man whom I had sat next to during our flight, who broke the silence. 'I think you are referring to the legend that King Arthur sleeps under Mount Etna, waiting for the time when he is needed to be of service to the British Isles again.' He spoke directly to Dottie who stared mutely back at him. 'I used to teach English literature; my particular interest is mediaeval, Elizabethan, the usual stuff, Shakespeare, Chaucer, Malory.' He paused, waiting to see if anyone else had anything to add but I think we were all still in shock at the turn the conversation had taken.

'Thomas Malory collected together various French and English myths and legends surrounding Arthur and his Knights of the Round Table,' he explained, 'and published them as his "Le Morte D'Arthur" in the fifteenth century, which was possibly written during his incarceration in Newgate Prison for political reasons.' Suddenly it seemed as if the whole room had fallen silent, waiting to hear what Patrick would say next. Dottie continued to sit as if she was a coiled spring waiting to be released. I thought Millie was holding her breath. Tom and Angela, the couple I had spoken to on the gorge walk, were leaning eagerly towards Patrick, expressions of rapt attention on their faces.

I was as interested as any British child who grew up reading about the tales of Arthur and his Knights, especially as we were due to visit Etna the next day but looking around at my fellow travellers with their eyes glittering with excitement, mouths open a little in wonder, I pondered whether I had accidentally booked onto some Arthurian fanatics holiday, the sort that have conventions and where participants dress up in costumes; a thought that had me wondering if anyone had packed his knightly doublet and hose for our farewell banquet on the last night. Were any of the women planning on masquerading as a damsel in distress hoping to be rescued?

I peered around at my companions, most who it seemed belonged to the "grey brigade"; I wondered if some of the stories I had heard about them were true? Vanessa and I seemed to be the odd ones out, being much younger.

I dragged my attention back to what Patrick was saying. 'When Arthur was injured at the battle of Camlann he was taken by boat to recover on the Isle of Avalon, where his fabled sword Excalibur had been forged. Most people identify Glastonbury Torr as Avalon but there is also the suggestion it might have been Sicily. In those days, as now, compared to cold, grey, rainy Britain, Sicily was an island of mystery, and with its warmer climate it equated to the paradise where the dead normally departed. The Vikings went to Valhalla, Arthur went to Avalon.'

'So therefore Excalibur was forged in Mount Etna?'

queried Millie.

Patrick glanced towards Dottie who still remained silent, then nodded. 'The story goes that the sword was forged in Avalon and therefore if Avalon is Sicily then Mount Etna would be the likely location of the forge. Or possibly Vulcano, which is one reason why I decided to make this trip, to be able to climb not one but two volcanos; not many tours of Sicily include a break on the Aeolian Islands, so we jumped at the chance.' Beside him his wife nodded agreement and there were similar murmurings among the group regarding staying on for the optional extension at the end of the tour of a few nights on the island of Vulcano.

'Of course, continued Patrick, 'Etna is not the only link with the Arthurian legend; there's the castle which we visit in a couple of days' time I think.' He looked to his wife for confirmation. 'But I am getting a little ahead of myself. The story goes,' I noticed a little smile as he knew he had his audience hooked, and he continued in the clear voice of a person used to public speaking, 'that the sister of Richard the First, the Lionheart, her name was Joan or Joanne, had been married to King William the Second of Sicily and then been imprisoned by the new King, Tancred for some reason, probably no more than the fact that she was the widow of his predecessor. On his way to the Holy Land Richard stopped off at Sicily and attempted to secure her release. Now, he also wanted to marry his nephew Arthur of Brittany, who was four years old at the time, to one of Tancred's daughters. Don't ask me how old the girl was,' he said forestalling Millie's next question, 'as I don't know. Anyway, to seal the bargain Arthur was reported to have given Tancred Excalibur, which was the Sword in the lake; other sources say that the Sword in the Stone, Caliburn, may have been the gift. Some people are surprised to learn that Arthur had more than one sword; as a king I would be surprised if he had only two.'

Here Patrick chuckled, assuming, probably quite rightly that most of those people gathered around him were only aware of Excalibur as Arthur's sword. Dottie looked like she was going to interrupt him or correct him but then thought better of it.

'Tancred may have been duped into believing that the sword he had been given was the genuine article, and many Sicilians believe that it was hidden in the walls of Tancred's palace, where it remains to this day. It was reported that Henry the Second, the father of Richard and Joanne, found the sword in Glastonbury with the graves of Arthur and Guinevere, although what became of those graves is not known, and, of course, Henry could have then passed the sword down to his son. The question is – which palace was "Tancred's palace."' Another smile. 'Of course, a palace in those days may have been what we would describe more as a "castle."'

'The castle we are visiting in a day or two?' asked Tom. 'Do you suppose it could be that one, Tancred's Palace?'

'Aci Castello,' supplied Dottie glaring at Patrick as if he had just given away state secrets.

Angela, Tom's wife, started flicking through her guidebook. 'Here it is,' she announced. 'It's not very big. Built of lava by the Normans in ten seventy-six.' She turned a few more pages. 'There is another castle in Palermo, or rather a Royal Palace; that sounds more promising,' she giggled. '"During Norman times it was the seat of the Kings of Sicily," it says.'

'That sounds more like it,' Tom agreed, and the rest of us nodded, as if this tour had suddenly become a giant treasure hunt.

Angela continued to read from her guide book. '"These days it is used by the Sicilian government for parliamentary business but parts of the Royal Apartments are open to the public during the week." Are we going there, dear?'

'I don't think it is part of our scheduled itinerary,' her husband replied, 'but we might be able to fit it in during our free time, depending on exactly where it is.' Angela unfolded the map at the back of the book, and she and Tom leaned over it, talking in low voices as they planned a possible excursion. I noticed Dottie trying to peer over her shoulder.

There was a lull in the conversation as the barman appeared and removed a couple of empty glasses. Patrick took the opportunity to order another beer and likewise Vanessa, with a beaming smile bestowed on the young man, asked if he could possibly bring her another glass of his excellent white wine, as if he trod the grapes himself during his free time.

'Etna is also known as *Mongibello* or *Montebello* meaning "beautiful mountain," resumed Dottie, foiled in her tentative map reading, and suddenly reanimated. 'Now *Mongibel* is the name of the otherworld castle of Morgan Le Fey, and her half-brother, Arthur. It was situated at Etna, according to the old Breton minstrels who accompanied the Normans when they occupied Sicily. Indeed, in ancient stories Morgan is called the "Fairy of Etna."'

Paul cleared his throat a little nervously pre-paratory to adding his contribution to the discussion. Instantly heads turned towards him like spectators at a tennis match. 'The Straits of Messina between Sicily and mainland Italy have over the centuries been the source of tales of mirages over the water, called "Fata Morgana" similar to mirages in the desert; whole cities have been reflected onto the horizon of the waters.'

Christine leaned towards Millie and I heard her whisper, 'Science teacher,' while her husband continued his lecture, more confidently now he felt assured of his audience's attention. 'These mirages were named after Morgan Le Fey due to her ability to conjure up illusions, such as when she reportedly hid the Lake, the home of the Lady of the Lake, and it was further said that she conjured up false images on the water in order to lure sailors to their deaths.'

'Like the Sirens in the Odyssey?' Millie asked.

'Yes, in a way; the Sirens lured sailors with their singing, whilst Morgan used images of fake land; the end result was the same. I can tell you the science behind it, if you like,' he added in a hopeful voice that we might beg him to inform us; Millie dutifully obliged while Vanessa, none too successfully, stifled a yawn.

'Well then, these mirages can be seen over water or in the desert and even in polar regions. They can fluctuate and change, be upside down and even stacked one on top of each other, or appear stretched out or distorted in some way. This happens when rays of light are bent as they pass through layers of air of different temperatures,' he waved his arms about as if demonstrating light bending, 'when air above is significantly warmer than the air below. Now, air is normally warmer nearer the surface and cooler higher up. In calm weather, warmer air may rest over cooler denser air forming an atmospheric duct -' I glanced across at Millie to see if she was ingesting all of this; she appeared spellbound. '-that acts like a refractory lens producing a series of inverted and erect images. A Fata Morgana requires an atmospheric duct to be present, which only occurs if there is first a thermal inversion.'

Paul paused a second and gazed around his audience to judge whether he should continue. As he still had everyone's attention, excepting that of Vanessa whose eyes were following the movement of the young barman, he resumed, 'A Fata Morgana is one explanation of ghost ships seen at sea, such as the Flying Dutchman. These ships are seen at a distance and often emanate an eery glow,' he again waved his hands, this time illustrating an eery glow.

The barman re-appeared with the drinks. Vanessa smiled at him again as her glass was placed before her and then nodded towards Paul muttering in an undertone, 'I bet his class love him.'

'Often the phenomenon causes ships to appear as if they are suspended in air,' Paul continued, well into classroom mode. 'It also gave rise to phantom islands in times when map making was in its infancy, particularly in artic or Antarctic regions when land masses were named, only to be later proved not to exist. The phenomenon may also be responsible for some UFO sightings when images are seen hovering in the air.' Here Paul looked around the little group as if seeing whether there were any forthcoming requests for further details. I saw Millie open her mouth so promptly nudged her, none too gently in my haste, and turned feverishly groping for something to say to divert the conversation.

'So, is that it then?' I asked to anyone in general. 'Regarding the Arthurian sites in Sicily?' Maybe it was the wine, but I found myself suddenly strangely fascinated with the thought that a mythical king of England or Britain may have spent time in a foreign country or, at any rate, had left his mark on their culture. Besides, I had always much preferred history to science.

'In Sicily, possibly,' Dottie answered, 'but of course there are others, better connected such as, of course, Glastonbury being the main one.'

'You have been to many?' Hilary asked.

Dottie preened herself and replied, 'I am fortunate to have visited many of them, the most important ones certainly. Why, only last year I joined a tour of the West Country specifically touring Arthurian related sites.'

'Oh, like people who tour film location sites?' Vanessa asked her interest momentarily aroused. She tucked a stray strand of blond hair behind her ear as she leaned forward and said, 'I had a friend who came to Sicily last year and watched them filming *Inspector Montalbano*, that new series they showed on the BBC.'

I made a mental note to look out for the programme, just out of interest, in case they had filmed in any of the places we were due to visit. 'We went to Florence a few years ago,' I said, 'my sister and I. It was really hot, I mean really, really hot. We just happened to be passing as they were filming; a lady came out of the cathedral wearing a fur coat! She must have been sweltering.'

'Friends of ours went to Cornwall,' commented Hilary, Patrick's wife, 'just to see the places where *Poldark* was shot. One had had a tremendous crush on one of the actors after it was first shown, when was it? Nineteen seventy-three? Seventy-four? Anyway, she went on some mini tour to see the farmhouse where they lived and the big country house plus, of course, there are lots of nice places to visit in Cornwall anyway.' She paused before adding in a low voice, 'Patrick had hoped we would be visiting the hill top Mafia village of Corleone, and also the bar in Savoca where they filmed the *Godfather*. He's was rather hoping we might have been able to squeeze in a visit but I don't somehow think Mary is going to be very accommodating regarding extra excursions.' She paused before adding slightly disapprovingly, 'She doesn't seem too enamoured of the set schedule.' She gave a sigh of suppressed disappointment and picked up her wine glass.

We were in danger of having the conversation diverted to favourite television series and film locations in general and I was keen to hear more about the Arthur links so I asked Dottie if she had been to Dorset. 'When I was young we used to visit a place called Badbury Rings. It is an old Iron Age fort comprised of concentric rings, you know the type, banks and ditches. We used to have races down the hillsides on sheets of old canvas.' I felt myself colouring at the childhood memory. 'I read that it was a possible location of Mount Badon where Arthur fought his final battle.'

'Ah, Mount Badon,' Dottie repeated.

I nodded. 'It is reputed to be haunted, and at midnight Arthur and his knights return to relive his final battle, whereas other people claim it is the Romans who haunt the area.'

Beside me Millie suddenly giggled and said, 'I like a good ghost story!' However, Dottie seemed to think that the rest of us were not taking the subject as seriously as she was with talk about television programmes and ghosts. Only Patrick with his scholarly approach appeared to win her favour despite that being from a literary view. The scientific aspects Paul had presented had, I suspected, gone over her head, much as it had mine, only she hated to admit it. Bestowing a smile towards that favoured gentleman, which metamorphosed into a frown for the rest of us mere mortals, she announced that it was time she turned in. As she made her way across the bar I heard Millie ask, 'Into what, I wonder?'

Later, as Millie and I walked back to our respective rooms we reflected on the evening's discussion.

'Odd that Paul and Patrick are both school teachers,' I said. 'Though they are probably retired, otherwise they would be at school now, as I think this is term time.'

Millie considered this but thought that she had previously been on holiday with a group of people who turned out to be school or college lecturers, and on another trip various people all had a medical connection, nurses, porters, people that take blood, that sort of thing. Such coincidences happen, she decided.

'Do you believe those stories?' I asked her a little hesitantly, after all she was a new acquaintance and I did not want to offend her if she did, 'about Excalibur being forged in Etna and then hidden somewhere around here?'

She shrugged. 'Seems to me it doesn't matter what I think, but there are others who do believe it. And not just Dottie.'

'Who else?' I asked her in amazement.

'Tom and Angela for one, or two rather, they were very keen on finding out about the royal palace in Palermo, and Paul knew an awful lot about it for a school science teacher.'

'I wondered why you were encouraging him.'

'I felt sorry for him,' Millie admitted. 'He seemed so enthusiastic about his subject, someone had to listen and ask questions, and I rather got the feeling his scholars might not be so keen.'

'So that's three people,' I said, 'four, if you include Christine. No, five; mustn't forget Dottie'.

'Seven,' Millie corrected. 'You're forgetting Patrick and his wife. A tour of Sicily is not the tour I would have picked for a literary buff; he might just as well have gone to Verona.'

'There could be other reasons for taking a holiday. Maybe he has already been to Verona.'

'True,' Millie agreed.

Then a thought struck me. 'You think they really are teachers? I mean, he didn't just say he was a teacher, not expecting there to be any others in the group who could prove it was false; but why lie about a thing like that?'

Again Millie shrugged, then she giggled. 'It's fun though, isn't it? Thinking up all these reasons for other people's holidays. Going to be difficult in a couple of days' time, though,' she pointed out.

'Why?'

'How are we going to follow seven people around Aci Castello?'

Chapter Three

Up Mount Etna

One of the reasons I had booked this holiday was because very few other tours to Sicily offered a chance to visit Mount Etna, the active volcano that simply dominates the island. From just about any-where on Sicily you can tilt your head back and view the peak, sometimes ejecting whitish gas into the air. At the start of their stay visitors are obsessed with photographing it as a backdrop to just about every picture. However, after a few days the novelty seems to wear off and by the end of the week they act as blasé about it as the locals.

Some years earlier I had climbed up Mount Vesuvius, the volcano on mainland Italy whose eruption had destroyed both Pompeii and Herculaneum – okay, so you get taken half way up by coach – but I had then walked to the summit where

I could look down into its crater and also appreciate the views across the surrounding countryside. Therefore, I was keen to explore the heights the Sicilian volcano had to offer.

I slept a little better the second night and was up bright and early, eager to get started on the half day exploration. I had almost finished my breakfast when Mary approached me and without preamble pointed at my feet and announced, 'I don't think those are suitable wear for climbing up Etna.'

I looked down at my pale blue sandals, flat and sturdy, distinctly functional as opposed to fashionable, but open toed.

'I'm going up to change into my walking shoes after I have finished breakfast,' I explained, feeling a little like a naughty schoolgirl caught out of uniform. 'I only put these on now as I didn't want to get hot feet.'

Mary glanced down once more at my offending footwear before turning away to assess the suitability of Vanessa's shoes, a strappy pair of red leather sandals with a somewhat modest heel that made mine look positively dowdy. Vanessa, however declared she had no interest in mountain climbing but was going to find somewhere to sit and read her book. Mary turned on her heel and marched off, her back ramrod straight with an air of righteous indignation that her advice was being ignored while I exchanged a grin with Vanessa as we considered her officious manner.

We are adults on holiday, I thought. We can wear

43

what we like as long it does not offend the locals (such as covering shoulders in church) and wear high heeled shoes, if we can walk in them, and if we are not planning on walking up mountains.

However, despite exchanging pleasantries with Vanessa after her somewhat annoying behaviour yesterday, I was a little dismayed to hear she had decided she was not going to take the cable car up the mountain. I hoped a sizeable number of people were interested otherwise the opportunity might be withdrawn, as somehow I sensed that Mary was keen for a shortened excursion.

As if to tease us intrepid mountain explorers we did not drive straight to the volcano but made a slight detour on the way. My heart sank when we pulled into the car park at what appeared to be one of those money-making shopping stops that coach tours inflict on their patrons with varying levels of success. On one previous holiday we stopped so frequently at these outlets that it became a running joke that the tour leader must have been related to the store owners; however it is usually acknowledged that there is some sort of incentive, perhaps on a commission basis, for us travellers to have these "opportunities" thrust upon us; very rarely are many purchases made and often they are merely used as an excuse to use the retailers' washroom facilities.

This particular enterprise promoted locally produced honey. Once inside we were given a little talk about the produce and the range of items on offer but most importantly we had an opportunity to sample the wares. Despite it being not long since breakfast we managed to generate appetites and tasted not only a variety of flavoured honeys but also another stock product, liquors, although these were not so generously distributed however, but I repeat, it was not long since breakfast and perhaps a little early to be imbibing much alcohol.

Also, I suspected we needed to keep clear heads for our trip up the mountain. While I doubted we would be reaching particularly high altitudes where the oxygen might be considered scarce, as when climbing Mount Everest, we were still novices at such exploits and would need to keep our wits about us. So while we were plied with a multitude of flavoured honeys we were rationed to one tiny thimble full of liquor each. I think it was perhaps the only such commercial stop where every person on the trip bought at least one item; the honey, if not the liquor, making perfect gifts for family and friends back home.

After our purchases were complete Mary teased us further by making a second stop on our way to Mount Etna. This time the coach parked by the side of the road and we all disembarked as instructed with our cameras at the ready. We safely lined up along the grass verge to take photographs of the volcano, again with belching little puffs of white smoke from its highest crater.

Then we trooped back onto the bus for the remainder of our journey. As we neared our destination visible evidence of previous eruptions lined the hillsides; various sized dollops of lava, the ruins of habitations and also one or two more substantial buildings, the homes of hardy souls who still lived in the shadow of the mountain, until finally we arrived.

I itched to get started – the sooner we set off the longer time we would have and the more of the mountainside we would be able to cover. However, Mary again gave a little speech enquiring as to how many people wanted to ride up in the cable cars and who wanted to stay on the lower levels with the few shops. I was disappointed to hear that she was not allowing us time to take a jeep ride to the summit, which would take another hour or so after we had undertaken the cable car journey.

Vanessa made a great show of stashing a large book into her bag before she alighted from the bus and made her way towards the cabins selling souvenirs. Joan was standing with Dottie while the latter chatted away. I made my way towards the cable car ticket office and once there joined the end of the long queue of tourists.

As luck would have it, Paul and Christine were just ahead of me and after I had paid my fare they beckoned me forwards and asked if I would like to share a gondola with them, to which I eagerly agreed. A few minutes later, just as we were about to take our seats, Christine spotted Milly dithering about further back in the queue and she called to her, urging her to sit with us, four being the optimal number in each compartment, with one person sat in each corner to evenly distribute the weight. We had a slightly sticky moment when Millie, finding it difficult to hear with the vociferous crowds outside waiting to board, moved into the empty middle seat to hear Christine more clearly and the gondola rocked alarmingly until we urged her back into the corner and it stabilised once more.

The ride up the side of the volcano was nail bitingly slow. Every now and then, as the gondola came to some sort of junction, it jumped a fraction. At first I gazed out the windows at the view but as the ground receded and we passed over yawning chasms I decided to concentrate on my fellow companions instead. Conversation was stilted due to the bumps and accompanying slight swing of the gondola and I don't think I was the only person nervously gripping the edge of the seat. I heaved a huge sigh of relief when we reached the end of the ride and alighted carefully, the gondola again swinging perilously as each person moved to get out and its load lightened.

Once out in the open we briefly stretched our legs and orientated ourselves for the next part of the ascent. We strolled at a reasonable pace, I think in deference to Millie's advanced age and slightly shorter legs although she at times marched ahead only to get side tracked by the view or an interesting lump of rock. After a while we checked our watches; Mary had given us time for a stroll but we also needed to eat before we reboarded the bus. There was a café at the point where we disembarked the cable car and so we elected to eat there as opposed to waiting until we returned back down to the car park area and the souvenir stalls; I assumed there was somewhere to eat for Mary, Vanessa and the others who had elected not to venture up the volcano.

'Just a bit further, I think,' Paul suggested. 'See what's around the next bend.'

We agreed, however, around the next bend the landscape looked pretty similar, dark boulders of varying sizes bordering the pathway. The view over the surrounding countryside was unfortunately obscured by haze. We walked on. A couple of jeeps drove past us taking people to the summit.

All around us we spied tiny ladybirds that had been caught in rising air thermals and then become trapped on the mountainside.

I strode on a little further but the landscape appeared a monotonous monochrome of black lava, the trail grit in varying shades of grey; it was the same all around, in the end we decided it was time to turn back; there was nothing different to see.

While we had stopped to consider whether to continue or retrace our steps Millie had produced from her bag a bottle securely wrapped up in a linen scarf. Saying that the hot, dry air was playing havoc with her skin, and all the dust did not help, she applied some emollient to her arms, before re-wrapping the bottle and replacing it in her bag. I noted, though, that she wore long loose-fitting sleeves that completely covered her skin so I was a little unsure of her need for suntan lotion. Christine, however agreed that suntan lotion was essential and they discussed different level protection factor creams during the return walk back.

At the halfway station I managed to purchase rolls and a cup of tea in the little café, the queues of which seemed interminable and for some reason no matter who had been served I still seemed to be no nearer the front of the queue. We sat at solid plain wooden refectory tables and hungrily munched away.

I cast one eye on a television screen in the corner which showed a muted potted history of Etna with an accompanying graphic explanation of various eruptions. Out of habit I stared at the screen for a few moments, reading the subtitles: *Etna is the highest volcano in Europe and one of the most active in the world. Its summit has four craters.*

As tour groups tend to do in such situations we congregated in one section of the dining area, our little party from last evening but minus Vanessa and with the addition of the Americans, Don and his wife, Cherie, and indeed, after most had finished eating after their strenuous (or otherwise) exercise, conversation seemed to pick up on the same thread.

'So, after our little walk around do we believe that the forge of Hephaestus – or Vulcanus, to give him his Latin or Roman name – is somewhere underneath us?' Patrick asked.

The smiles this provoked broadened when Millie asked, 'Is there any connection with the Vulcans in *Star Trek* I wonder?'

'Well, they live on a hot planet,' suggested Don.

'I doubt anyone is suggesting that the ancient

Greek or Roman gods had deformed ears,' Paul commented, 'after all, I thought that most gods, and not just the Christian one, made Man in his own image.' There was a general nodding of heads as we considered this.

I popped the last of my chicken salad roll into my mouth then slurped some tea while my eyes strayed once more to the TV set in the corner, which had restarted its loop again and was showing guided walks of the area: *In summer there are hiking trails through Etna Park, through woods and orchards grown on its rich fertile soils, to view the lunar landscapes, ancient lava flows and active fumaroles. In winter it is possible to ski, both downhill and cross country in the vicinity.*

'And not just the master forger – oh that sounds wrong,' Paul added, 'makes him sound like some criminal boss and not a blacksmith!'

'You were thinking Mafia,' Don teased amid generalised laughter.

'Anyway,' Paul sighed and continued, 'apparently it is not just the blacksmith working in his forge deep under the volcano, but according to Greek mythology the deadly monster Typhon fought Zeus for supremacy of the gods and when he lost he was supposedly trapped by Zeus under Etna.'

As if in comment there was a large explosion from the television in the corner. Beside me Millie jumped and spilled a little of her tea.

'Goodness!' she exclaimed. 'I had no idea there was a television set in the corner.' She giggled. 'Have I missed anything?'

'It's just a sort of mini documentary on the volcano,' I informed her. 'It keeps repeating on a loop. *The earliest recorded eruption was in 396 BC, with a second in 122 BC. There were further eruptions in 1160 or possibly 1224 –*

'Were those Norman times?' Millie asked.

I shrugged. 'I'm not sure offhand.' After some more consideration I added, 'But the Battle of Hastings was ten-sixty-six, and that was between William the Conqueror and King Harold Something-or-other, which marked the Norman Invasion of England, so a bit later.'

Millie nodded her agreement and we turned our attention back to the TV screen.

An eruption in 1669 was the most destructive since 122 BC and destroyed 10 villages and reached Catania five weeks later. Lava was diverted by the city walls into the sea, and although there was extensive damage to property no deaths were reported. However, a further eruption in 1693 may have been responsible for possibly 20,000 deaths. Studies have confirmed that only 77 deaths have been recorded with certainty, the most recent being in 1987 when 2 tourists near the summit were killed by a sudden explosion. In 2008 an eruption caused the airport in Catania to close due to falling ash. Several recent eruptions have resulted in damage to the cable car -

Millie and I exchanged worried glances.

'I think perhaps it's time we left,' she suggested.

This time during our journey in the cable car, as the ground became nearer and the drop if we were to fall less, I took more interest in our descent, and even managed to take a couple of snaps, although one at least was blurry as I mistimed my shot and snapped away just as the cable car went over one of the pylons with a jolt. Then we were back on solid earth and I wandered off in search of (another) shopping opportunity.

There was a long queue in what appeared to be the official gift shop, possibly as there did not seem to be anyone serving at the counter, so I abandoned the idea of buying any postcards with stamps from that outlet and wandered outside to peruse the various stalls.

I have discovered over the time that I have been travelling that the quality of merchandise on offer at roadside stalls varies considerably, as do the corresponding prices. I have come across the usual vendors offering poorly constructed tat unlikely to survive the journey home offered at remarkably expensive prices, presumably as anyone who buys is desperate for that last minute gift; but there has also been the occasional stall selling unusual, often unique items of good quality for very reasonable prices; the sort of items that you say to yourself 'I have not got time to buy it now but I am bound to see another like it in the next town.' But you never do and you spend the rest of your holiday berating yourself and saying 'next time I see something I like at a reasonable price – I will buy it!'

Therefore, I joined the throngs of sightseers milling around the cabins bordering the car park and, as ever, gravitated to the one that appeared to be selling alcohol, although one glance at the bottles on sale was enough to confirm that I was not tempted to buy, not in the least. Consequently, I was surprised to see two of my fellow travellers seemingly in the process of making a purchase, but as the saying goes, "one man's meat is another man's poison."

The bottles offered for sale by the stall holder were similar to those I had briefly glimpsed in town yesterday, the sort that once seen you could not forget due to their hideous nature. Each bottle was encrusted with various sized lumps of black volcanic rock, some "tastefully" covered in small chippings, others seemingly thrust into chunks so that they appeared to be emerging like Aphrodite, or perhaps more appropriately, the Roman Venus, from her shell. Most of the bottles appeared to contain red wine although some were labelled "fire water."

Someone edged up beside me, nudged me in my side and queried, 'Brandy do you suppose? Or whisky?'

I turned and saw Vanessa indicating a monstrous looking bottle clad in the lava chippings complete with a drawing of a rather rudely suggestive erupting volcano on its label.

'Drain cleaner?' I offered in reply. Judging by their dusty and begrimed state many of the items seemed to have been sitting on the stall open to the elements for quite some time; perhaps the seller thought that just added a worn authenticity to their appearance. 'You're not buying?' I added a little incredulously and then wished I had not sounded like I thought buying such tat was beneath me, however I inwardly breathed a sigh of relief when she flapped her hand at me replying, 'Gawd, no!' and we both laughed. However, I almost choked when she pointed to the couple further along adding, 'But they are.'

I peered around her and recognised an older couple who I had briefly spoken to in the bar last night, Tom and Angela, about the gorge walk. He had done 95% of the talking and she had smiled and nodded and agreed with any sentiment he had expressed. Both were impeccably dressed in casual slacks and polo necked T-shirts and even now, after our trip up the volcano they looked clean and neat and tidy, whereas my trainers were covered in dust, and my hair had started to come loose from its band; little wisps kept flying around my face in the keen breeze.

I watched open mouthed as Tom contemplated several of the bottles, including those labelled "Fire Water." Not all the labels included pictures of Mount Etna erupting; several had maps portraying Sicily with "X" marking the spot of the volcano and others showed pictures of various ancient gods. Tom selected a medium sized bottled with a picture depicting a snake-like creature, muttered 'Typhon,' moved his head from side to side in a considering motion before replacing the bottle and asking the stall-holder, 'Hephaestus? No, no, Vulcan?'

The stall-holder, a large beefy looking man who certainly looked as if he ate lots of pasta, picked up and looked at in turn several bottles as if searching for the elusive god. Finally, he scratched his head before muttering, 'Aah' in a sort of 'Eureka!' moment and he disappeared behind the stall where judging by the noise he was rummaging in boxes. At last he emerged triumphantly holding aloft a bottle that looked new and untarnished, which he presented to Tom in the manner of a head waiter in an exclusive restaurant with the accompanying confirmation, 'Vulcano!'

Tom took the bottle as reverently as it was offered. He ran his finger down the label on the front which by craning my neck I saw depicted a statue of that god standing over an anvil with his hammer raised in his left hand. Tom nodded in confirmation before handing the bottle back to the vendor who proceeded to carefully wrap it in some bubble wrap.

'No, I would not buy one; with all that muck covering the bottle obscuring the contents it could contain almost anything,' I commented turning back to Vanessa, however I almost stopped in my tracks as a little behind her, carrying a motorcycle helmet, stood the man with grey curly hair I had noticed yesterday. I stared hard for a second or two. Despite the man wearing leathers in the warm weather it certainly looked like the person I had not been able to stop thinking about since. He too had been watching Tom buying his tourist bottle; when that purchase was completed he turned slightly and our eyes met. I immediately felt myself flush with embarrassment at being caught out staring at him.

Chapter Four

A Sicilian in Catania

In the microcosm that exists around a touring holiday when you are in close proximity to those who just a day or two earlier were complete strangers, unlikely friendships can develop, sometimes simply lasting for the duration of the holiday, occasionally for a longer period; an aunt of mine had remained in email contact with people whom she had met on one particular holiday for over ten years, people from such diverse locations as America, New Zealand and India.

There will always be people with whom you associate but never really get to know, such as the American couple, Don and his wife, Cherie, who hovered on the periphery of our group within the tour party, or people like Dilys whom whilst I knew her name I think I barely spoke to her more than once or twice during the entire holiday. There may even be people who keep themselves so distant from the rest of the tour group that you never discover their names let alone anything about them.

As you get to know your travelling companions people naturally fall into little clusters of people who you socialise with, although sometimes these might include people with whom you might rather not, such as Vanessa; while we spent time together I never really quite liked her and I don't think that was in any part due to jealousy on my part (or perhaps hers), but my first impression of her had not been favourable, and I should have trusted that more. Whilst my first impression of Millie was of an upright (in manner as well as deportment) little old lady, it took a couple of days to get beneath the veneer of self-preservation that we adopt on holiday.

Hence, as the days progressed and Millie and I got to know each other a little better, we relaxed more in each other's company. Age was no barrier; Millie might have been old enough to be my grandmother (possibly great grandmother, there was no necessity to find out her precise age) but we got along together and made suitable companions, keeping each other company and out of mischief – well I tried.

Our first visit of the day was to the nearby coastal town Castello di Aci, Mary had very little to say about the town, with its quaint Castello Normanno situated atop a large lump of volcanic rock overlooking the sea. The castle had been constructed of black lava stones taken from Mount Etna by Norman invaders in the eleventh century. As we drove along, however, Mary did point out that in the next village further along the coast are rocks that the Cyclops, the one-eyed giant of Greek legend, was supposed to have thrown at Odysseus when he and his men were escaping his clutches in their boat on their journey home from the Trojan War, but were presumably the result of volcanic eruptions. Millie had muttered, 'I rather prefer the Greek legend version,' and we exchanged grins.

Waiting outside for the man to open the entrance gates ('Sorry, ladies and gents, but in Italy opening times are merely suggestions, not to be taken as gospel truth that they *will* open at nine o'clock,' Mary had apologised) I gazed around and thought it was quite possibly the smallest, most compact castle I had ever seen.

After we had been hovering around for about twenty minutes a smiling man strolled up offering apologies. I was struck my his manner; he seemed genuinely pleased to have visitors to his tiny castle and sorry to have kept us waiting; if a similar situation had occurred in Britain doubtless the gate-keeper or warden would have covered any embarrassment in his lax timekeeping with bluster and attempts to make us feel in the wrong by turning up early.

Once inside we were then let loose to wander around, to view the limited number of inside rooms and then take a stroll about the picturesque and well-tended garden, best viewed from the battlements.

Millie was itching to get inside; not to view the interior, however but to start tailing her suspects.

'What are you expecting them to do?' I had asked her at breakfast, as she outlined her plan that she had first mentioned a couple of nights ago in which I found I had somehow been included. 'Rip the volcanic walls apart with their bare hands whilst searching for the sword?' However, she was undeterred.

'There must be gaps in the walls, especially after all these years. Is Sicily prone to earthquakes?' she had asked.

'I think any gaps in walls would have been found and explored long ago,' I argued. 'Even those occurring more recently due to seismic activity, vibrations from volcanic eruptions that sort of thing. There must be custodians of the castle, employed to ensure its upkeep and not just to take money from visitors and sell them postcards. Someone will be tending to the grounds, sweeping the floors and keeping them free from litter.'

Millie had been momentarily silenced but still adamant that she intended to follow her quarry and as I thought I better keep a protective eye on my octogenarian friend, that meant I would be tailing them as well. I had just wanted to enjoy the castle!

Luckily for such a small castle, and for those of us intent on surveillance, other than our group there was only one other couple with a small child who appeared after a while; obviously other people were aware of the flexible opening hours and had left their visits until later in the day, and so Millie was able to keep tabs on her quarry quite easily.

Unfortunately, Millie could not decide on whom she wanted to follow first, hence we ducked down behind parapets, dived around columns and corners, and hid behind huge cactus in the grounds. At one point I turned to Millie and told her, 'No-one is acting suspiciously; only us!' but she insisted we keep up our covert activities.

'Aren't you interested in whether someone is searching for the sword from the stone?' she hissed in reply. Then corrected herself, 'sword from the lake.' She paused and then muttered under her breath, 'sword from the lake, huh! It doesn't even rhyme. It should be "the chalice from the palace."'

I had no idea what she was muttering about and wondered, not for the first time, whether I was doing the right thing in letting such an old lady loose in a foreign country. Perhaps the heat was getting to be too much for her? Having befriended her, and as a fellow British woman travelling alone, I felt it was the "neighbourly" thing to do, to keep an eye on her; I would feel awful if something happened to her and I had done nothing to prevent it. I knew that was Mary's job but as she cannot be everywhere people who travel in tour groups normally look after each other. I looked around for some shade.

Noting my concerned frown, Millie explained, 'Danny Kaye, dear. Before your time. And look for evidence of secret passages and priest's holes.'

'Priest's holes?' I queried. 'This is a Norman castle.

They might have needed a secret passage as an escape route, or perhaps for smuggling, that sort of thing, but why should there be any Priest's holes? I think that's an English thing. Mary did not mention anything about the Spanish Inquisition here, only when we get to Palermo.'

When Dottie suddenly appeared we pretended to be interested in a cannon set into the battlements that was directed out to sea. We scurried along in her wake as she inspected the walls until Millie, peering over the parapet spied Paul and Christine in the gardens.

'That's where we should be,' she hissed and before I could stop her she was scampering down the stairs as fast as her arthritic joints could manage. I cast a glance back at Dottie, who was now intent on the cannon we had admired, before following Millie, more so as to keep a safe eye on her than any concern as to what Paul and Christine were up to among the flora.

Down in the grounds, amongst gravel strewn beds, grew many varieties of cactuses, some much taller than us, although in the case of Millie and myself, that is not particularly tall. Flowering varieties cascaded over the battlements and I suppressed a smile as to what the original builders might have made of these decorative features. It soon became apparent that Christine was more interested in plants than ancient weaponry and so Millie gazed about despondently until she spotted Patrick and Hilary strolling back into the bowels of the building.

'Quick!' Millie urged in a loud whisper and I duly followed, pausing to admire an ancient door of solid panelled wood. 'Yes, very nice,' Millie agreed giving it barely a second look. 'Come on! They're getting away!'

'Where can they go?' I asked a little exasperated. 'There are only about three rooms inside.' Nonetheless I trailed in her wake like an obedient chick behind its mother hen until she glimpsed Tom and Angela seated around a table in an outdoor rest area. Quickly she changed course, inched into an alcove and peered around the corner. Again I followed, and we stood, noses to the lava wall watching the couple doing nothing more sinister than relaxing in the shade, like two detectives from a B movie, when a voice behind us asked, 'Having fun ladies?'

I turned around to see the tall, lanky figure of Richard grinning at us. Whilst we had been stalking various people around the castle had Richard been keeping an eye on us?

Millie and I settled ourselves in our customary seats at the back of the bus a little sheepishly on the short journey to Catania. As we had slipped into position Richard had grinned once more at us and winked a greeting, 'Ladies!'

I turned to contemplate the scenery outside but my mind was racing – had Richard been following us all around the castle? I cast my mind back to the other evening and tried to remember if he had been present when we had discussed, well Richard, the other Richard, King of England. Had he participated in the conversation? Or possibly been a present but silent participant?

Millie had also turned her back on the man in embarrassment. He sat in between us on the back seat, legs stretched out up the aisle in order to lay claim to his position due to his height and long legs; none of the other tall men (or ladies for that matter) had challenged him on this and seemed happy to squeeze themselves into other places. No-one else had expressed a desire to sit on the back seat with him hence Millie and I had not rotated seats either; just for once I wished that we had.

Catania has been flattened and rebuilt many times due to numerous volcanic eruptions and natural disasters, most notably after the earthquake of 1693. Its first cathedral was built by the Normans – who else? in the eleventh century; its Baroque replacement, which we briefly viewed, incorporates columns from the nearby Roman amphitheatre. Only a portion of this area remains, which can still be seen below ground level. We walked around the section on display peering down at the tiered seats and steps constructed out of dark basalt Etna rock; it seemed odd to look down on something that when it was originally built would have loomed skywards, a testament presumably to the surrounding city being built on accumulated lava deposits from the nearby volcano.

Our brief tour of the town concluded with final instructions to meet back later in the afternoon at the Elephant statue, a lava sculpture with an Egyptian obelisk situated in the Piazza Duomo; we were thus set free to wander around the area and grab a bite to eat.

We – Joan, (I wondered why she was not with Vanessa – and where was Vanessa?) Millie and I - followed Mary's directions to *La Pescheria* in the southwest corner of the city. Despite the stench of fresh fish we spent some time in the fish market gawping at the specimens on display and watching the buying and selling, some of which looked none too hygienic. After spying a huge sword fish hung up on display Millie had a sudden desire to have her photograph taken standing next to it, then she declared that all this food made her feel suddenly hungry and we agreed it was time for lunch.

Despite there being several restaurants situated around the main square after a quick perusal of their menus we decided to search for something a little more downmarket; I did not want to splash out a huge amount on a midday meal until I was a little more used to the currency and exchange rates while both Millie and Joan professed to small appetites, and none of us wanted to drink wine during the day. I banished the thought that I was pleased Vanessa was not with us, with her two glasses of white wine and her attitude that she had all the time in the world to sit and chat (about herself). I imagined her eating in one of the posher restaurants with a glass in her hand;

well if that was the kind of holiday she wanted that was fine, but we three were happy to sit in a little road side café, eating homemade lasagne washed down by sparking spring water.

I think at this time, without the overbearing presence of Vanessa Joan was able to contribute a little more to the conversation, although Millie did most of the talking. We discovered that Vanessa had gone clothes shopping in the swanky boutique shops and that Joan, like myself, had had to change her travel plans, being originally destined to holiday in Syria. I looked at her afresh after this comment; while outwardly reticent she nevertheless possessed an inner strength illustrated not only by her willingness to holiday alone without her husband, who we discovered was a farmer and thus unwilling to leave his home for long periods of time, but also her inclination to travel to countries other more outgoing appearing people might shy away from.

'I did look at the Syria trip,' I admitted. 'It has several areas of historic interest but I thought the hotels a little uninspiring.'

'With all this Arab Spring business I doubt it has many attractions left,' Millie commented. Joan nodded agreement. 'It is a shame that we are losing many archaeological and cultural sites but living people must come first.' Again Joan nodded and I agreed. 'So, ladies, what's the plan for the rest of our free time?'

Tentatively I suggested we search for the Greek theatre. 'I know we've already seen one and doubtless due to see several more over the course of the next few days, but Catania does not seem to have the sort of gift shops that I would like to browse in. Also, we do still have two or three hours left to fill.'

My companions agreed and we went in search of the ancient ruins, which according to Mary's instructions, were tucked away up a side street. From its modest entrance area you would never guess that in the midst of all the Baroque buildings lies such an extensive archaeological area dating from the first century AD, which was perhaps only slightly smaller than the one we had visited in Taormina.

We climbed the massive stone steps to view the stage area and strolled along its walkways. Around the back of the area we discovered some modern blue portoloos (locked) but in place ready to be used, as it seems the theatre, like so many, is still in use today for occasional concerts.

At one side the building backed onto normal every day houses and I wondered what it would be like to live next door to an ancient monument; like setting up house next to Stonehenge. A short distance away was the Odeion, a smaller theatre, where poetry and musical contests were held and it was also used as a rehearsal area for the main Theatre. As with most other buildings much of the construction material for the sites was lava.

I looked at my watch and was surprised to see we still had a little free time so we casually made our way back towards the town centre via what appeared to be in a residential area. We had not walked far when

Millie spotted a rather grand house in a faded sort of way set back from the roadside. A high wall surrounded the property, with large gates, which were open through which we spied a courtyard area surrounding a fountain.

'That look's nice!' Joan said, and before I could stop her she had strolled through the gateway and was admiring the fountain in what was probably private property.

Horrified, I looked at Millie who shrugged her shoulders and then we both hurried in as discretely as possible to try and persuade Joan that perhaps it was not a good idea to wander around someone else's property while on holiday in a foreign country, even if the gates were open as if to entice people to walk inside. I had no idea about Italian laws on trespass.

As luck would have it, although the courtyard had looked inviting from the street, once inside other than the fountain there was little to see; a few planters containing shrubs and plants in various stages of decay so that it was difficult to distinguish their species. I hoped that perhaps the property was vacant and no-one would notice us trespassing.

With Millie on one side of Joan and me on the other we managed to usher her back through the opening as speedily as we could. I was glancing over my shoulder back towards the building, just to check that we were not being watched from within, when we reached the pavement and I almost collided with a man riding a pushbike, who was himself in the process of turning in through the gates.

He pulled up sharply with a screech of brakes and I lifted my eyes from the wheels, which had suddenly stopped spinning, up into a pair of twinkling brown eyes set in a tanned face surrounded by a mop of grey curls.

'Oh!' I cried out involuntarily.

With his feet planted firmly on the ground either side of the pedals he leaned forwards, concern etched across his handsome features.

'You are alright?' he asked. 'Did I run over your foot?'

I shook my head. I was finding it hard to find my voice. I realised I was staring at him and felt myself flush.

'You are alright? he repeated, releasing one hand from the handlebars and reaching out towards me in a tentative gesture.

I swallowed hard and found my voice. 'I'm fine, thank you,' I said politely. 'Just taken by surprise, that's all.'

'Surprise?' he queried. He had a pleasant voice, just the right side of deep and spoke clear, slightly accented English. 'You are surprised to see me? Here?' He looked just like he had when I had first spotted him two days ago in Taormina, although now he was frowning.

'Surprised to see anyone,' I tried to explain. 'I wasn't looking where I was going, and then we were going out and you were coming in.' I stopped, as he was looking at me as if I was not making any sense.

At this point Millie, who had been standing

silently with Joan, decided to intervene. 'Everyone is fine, no-one is injured. Just a case of a near collision, but no harm done,' she declared. I nodded agreement and that being sorted he smiled, a broad smile that lit up his handsome features. 'You live here?' Millie asked the man. 'This is your house? We are sorry if we are trespassing but the gates were open and we just wanted a peek.'

'My house? I live here?' For a second he looked confused. 'Ah! No, I was just riding in to turn around,' he explained. 'I am trespassing too.' He grinned and we all shared this little joke. Then for a second no-one spoke or moved. We stood motionless in the gateway blocking the entrance.

'Ladies,' he declared. 'I am Enzo – let me show you Catania!'

There was a minute or two of silence then Millie and Joan mumbled something together before Millie declared that her feet hurt and that she was tired of mooching around the streets. The two older ladies would sit in a café and watch the world go by. Joan, as ever, nodded silently in agreement.

'But you go, Carrie,' she urged me. 'I am sure this fine young man,-' at which point he grinned as if agreeing with her description, '- can show you something a little off the beaten track.'

I looked suspiciously at her, wondering if she meant what I thought she did, but she gazed innocently back at me. I was surprised at her suggestion that I go sightseeing with a complete stranger, handsome though he may be. Meanwhile,

Enzo announced, 'The cathedral, let me show you our wonderful cathedral!'

I explained that we had viewed the cathedral as part of our city tour earlier. I was loath to leave the two older women alone in a strange, sprawling city. I had no idea how old Joan was, possibly in her sixties or seventies and Millie, while she had aged well – after all she had come alone on a foreign holiday – looked to be a decade older, and having agreed to accompany them on a walk I did not now want to abandon them after the first pretty face made me a "better" offer. However, I did Enzo a disservice in my opinion of him.

'In that case,' he proclaimed, 'we will all sit and drink coffee, and watch the world go by,' adding that he knew the perfect place! Not too far, he advised Millie with a smile.

So, with Enzo pushing his bicycle, we walked a short distance to a quaint café, which was just as he had a promised, within easy walking distance. He appeared on good terms with the proprietor and acquired the best outside table for us; not too near the dusty curb side and the passing traffic, and on the opposite side of the frontage to a group of students busy laughing and smoking, but with a pleasant view down the street.

Enzo further treated us to creamy Sicilian ice-cream, and as I sat and ate a delicious pistachio flavour I attempted to observe him discretely. I decided he was, as I had already surmised, younger than his greying hair suggested. Despite being tanned due to living under a stronger sun his skin was unlined, except for some laughter lines around his eyes, and his brown eyes were clear.

At the café he chatted as much to Millie and Joan as he did to me, in fact I have a sneaking suspicion that somehow he managed in a gentlemanly manner to divide his time between us equally into three. He asked us about ourselves, but not in an intrusive way; more as a Sicilian curious about the English way of life. What were we doing here? Why had we chosen Sicily for our holiday and why this particular tour? He was surprised to discover that prior to this trip that the three of us had never met before; he somehow, perhaps by my reluctance to leave the other ladies by themselves, had gained the impression that we were old friends or possibly related, such as, he suggested two aunts and their niece.

However, other than explaining that "Enzo" was short for "Lorenzo" he volunteered very little information about himself and managed to evade all Millie's rather probing personal questions.

It was very pleasant and all too soon it was time to go as we needed to locate the elephant statue and meet up with the main group. Enzo, of course, knew the quickest and easiest route, and leaving his bicycle temporarily chained up at the café, he walked with us to the square.

'Did you know that in ancient times there used to be dwarf elephants in Sicily?' Enzo smiled as we shook our heads. I tried to imagine such a creature but all I could picture were baby elephants and Dumbo. 'It has been suggested that the ancient Greeks when they found the skulls of these elephants, which are about twice the size of a human skull and have a large central nasal cavity-'

'For the trunk,' suggested Millie.

'For the trunk,' Enzo agreed. 'The Greeks, they thought that these skulls belonged to giants who only had one eye *e eccoti* they called these Cyclops.'

'How fascinating!' Millie exclaimed. She beamed at the taller man who as he walked had shortened his stride to match hers. I could tell she was taken with him, his easy-going manner and Mediterranean charm, not to mention his handsome features. And she was not the only one; Joan had almost come alive at the café when he asked her where she was from and he had extracted more personal information from her (she was from the Home Counties, had two sons, five grandchildren and here she had produced a wallet containing their photographs which Enzo had duly admired, and an assortment of animals both pets and livestock, living on a farm as she does) in a few minutes than Millie and I had in the preceding two or three days.

And I admit that I was not immune to his charisma. I wanted to say, 'I saw him first!' and lay claim to him like a lovesick adolescent.

'And there is an elephant skeleton in the Catanian Museum of Minerology, Palaeontology and Vulcanology if you have the time to see it.' He looked around hopefully that we might agree. 'Or if you have a little longer than this afternoon, there is another in Milano.' Both Millie and Joan giggled like schoolgirls. He looked at me and asked, 'You would not like to spend some time in Milano with me?'

I did not know what to say. I was tempted but…My mind was whirling; while I had explained away to myself his presence in the amphitheatre after I had first spied him in Taormina as being part of the normal itinerary for someone visiting that area I was a little more hesitant to ascribe his being at Etna to this same theory, but (almost literally) bumping into him today (whilst I had hoped to see him again), for the third day running was, I felt, stretching coincidence just that little bit too far.

'Oh!' he said taking my silence to mean "no". 'There's my answer. È la vita.' He gave an expressive shrug then turned to share a grin with the other two ladies as if it was some private joke from which I was excluded. I was a little surprised at how quickly the older women had taken to this native Sicilian; he undoubtedly had charm but having only just met him, we really knew nothing about him, and while my heart was pounding my head was urging caution.

Our meeting time for the group was 4.30pm and at 4.28pm we were just approaching the elephant sculpture with Enzo leading the way when a female voice cried out:

'Oh! I just knew I would see you again!'

I watched in dismay as Vanessa detached herself from the group waiting at the base of statue and flung her arms around his neck in greeting.

Chapter Five

Stormy Weather

Dinner was a slightly strained affair that evening. We were seated around large circular tables and while I tried to avoid both Dottie and Vanessa for different reasons, it was inevitable, that as it was still only early days in our holiday and we were yet to get to know everyone, that people tended to stick with those with whom they had so far become acquainted. Therefore, I ended up on a table with both these ladies, as well as Millie, Joan, and Paul and Christine. Completing the number were the American couple, Don and his wife, Cherie.

'I sure am looking forward to the cathedral visit tomorrow,' Don announced, as we waited for our plates to be cleared between courses. 'I hear the mosaics in Cefalu and also in the cathedral in Monreale are very similar to the ones in the Hagia Sophia, in Istanbul. Have you been to Istanbul,

Carrie?'

I admitted that I had. 'The Hagia Sophia was one of the places I particularly wanted to visit having seen it in documentaries on TV. It was amazing,' I enthused.

'And also I am keen to see the cathedral in Syracuse. It was built around an ancient Greek temple; did you know that?' Don looked around the table at each of his fellow diners as if inviting comments. 'I am very interested in such places, like the Hagia Sophia, that have changed, adapted if you will, to different situations. The Hagia Sophia was a Christian church, then a mosque and is now a museum. The cathedral in Syracuse has been used for worship by various religions, first by the Greeks in their temple, then the Christians; it was also briefly a mosque as well before reverting back to Christian use.'

'I think that's true of many churches around the world,' said Paul. 'Look at Temple Mount in Jerusalem. It's a holy site for Jews, Christians and Muslims.'

Don nodded. 'Just what makes a site holy or sacred for many different people I wonder? Some places like those in Israel have so much history, but for all those churches and other structures that have maintained their special meaning, without any one event to base it on, as such; I mean, look at the Greek Temple in Syracuse – why was it built on that exact spot? And then why was it converted into a church?'

'Because people were used to worshiping there?'

suggested Millie. 'And also, as the structure was already standing, it was cheaper to build around it, to incorporate it into the design.'

'But if you wanted to move people away from one religion to another,' Don argued, 'if you were an invading army, for example, wouldn't you want to demolish the existing religious building and then in order to disassociate with the old religion, build afresh in a new location?'

'Maybe speed was of the essence if they wanted somewhere to pray,' Paul said.

Don considered this, but then shook his head. 'No, I think the important thing is the site, the land on which the building is situated.'

There was a momentary pause while one waiter removed our plates while a second gathered together unused cutlery and side plates.

'You mean Ley lines?' asked Dottie, her voice unnaturally loud in the silence that followed after the staff had finished tidying our table and moved onto the next. 'Lines of supernatural energy?'

Despite my intention to try and avoid Vanessa I saw her turn to Joan and whisper something which made the older woman smile.

'That's a possibility, of course,' Don conceded. 'Religious structures being built at the junction where such lines meet.'

'There's a church near where I live,' I said a little hesitantly, not wanting to set Dottie off on a tangent. 'Knowlton Church. It's a ruined Norman church,' I grinned at Millie, 'but it was built in the middle of

Neolithic earth rings which, I think, are pagan.'

'That's interesting,' Don said, momentarily forgetting his manners and putting his elbows on the table to lean closer. 'Of course, there's that other famous goddess' merger in Sulis Minerva at your Bath spa; Sulis being the Celtic goddess of health and healing waters, and Minerva being the Roman goddess of wisdom and the arts.'

I caught Millie's eye; I thought we were in danger of drifting into dangerous, if sacred, waters and I did not want to give Dottie an excuse to lecture on about Ley lines, swords in lakes and other possible nonsense.

As a waiter re-appeared Millie took my queue and said loudly, 'Ah, dessert, tiramisu, my favourite.' However, later she told me she could not stand the stuff, but could think of nothing else to say.

I decided I did not want to hang around and socialise in the bar after dinner, and using the excuse that I had yet to pack my case ready for our onward move tomorrow to Palermo I retired early.

Having only unpacked the bare necessities in the premise that there was then less to repack and possibly lose, it did not take long before I was sat on my bed, twiddling my thumbs. I did not want to watch Italian TV nor did I feel like reading my book. I felt neither tired nor in need of sleep. I was unsure why, but I felt, flat, deflated, for some reason this holiday had already lost some of its appeal.

My mind kept replaying various events from earlier in the day – when I had almost collided with Enzo cycling into the courtyard just as we had been leaving it; our chat at the little café when he had seemed so charming; and then the incident when Vanessa had flung herself at him. There was no other way to describe it; on seeing him she had positively leapt in his direction. He had appeared as surprised and shocked as the rest of us and had quickly, but gently tried to disentangle her arms from around his neck, whilst trying to persuade her that she had made a mistake; she had obviously confused him with someone else.

She had briefly postured and pouted, but had allowed him to extricate himself after which, with a fleeting glance it seemed of apology towards Millie, Joan and myself, he had made a hasty exit. I was unsure of what he felt he needed to apologise for – he was not responsible for Vanessa's behaviour surely, unless it was his speedy departure he regretted.

I had embarked on this holiday in order to relax and also to meet new people, see some of the country's historical sites, experience some Mediterranean culture, not to meet anyone in particular or embark on a holiday romance that was doomed to die away once I returned home; so why was I feeling so upset?

But as I lay awake in bed tossing and turning as sleep was elusive I heard again Vanessa's throw away comment of, 'Well, it was worth a try!' as we had watched him depart. However, my brain kept questioning – did they know each other? Had they met before?

And also, why when we were having our little chat at the café had Enzo not mentioned seeing us previously? I was unsure if he has seen us in Taormina or the amphitheatre but he had definitely seen us at Mount Etna, as I remembered our eyes meeting across the tourist stand.

I eventually fell into a fitful sleep where I dreamt that I was wandering around Catania with Millie and a pygmy elephant. After completing a circuit of the ruins of the ancient amphitheatre and returning to the main square, however where the fish market should be we turned towards the Norman castle of Aci Castello where we were engaged in a search for Richard, but whether it was tall, lanky Richard or the ancient King of England was unclear. After hunting through the grounds we attempted to enter the building only to be chased away by a huge cyclops on the battlements, with long straggly blond hair that looked suspiciously like Vanessa, throwing large lava boulders shouting, 'He's mine! I saw him first!'

The next day after breakfast we drove northwards to the coastal city of Cefalu where after a rather brief orientation tour of the town, the highlight being its twelfth century Norman cathedral, (here Millie's ears pricked up like a bloodhound on the trail of its prey), containing byzantine mosaics, Mary gave us free time to roam around.

Millie needed no urging to step inside the cathedral, with its imposing towers on either corner at the front. The interior was dark and gloomy, and I felt myself drawn to the golden mosaic of Jesus Christ above the main altar, indeed similar to that in the Hagia Sophia in Istanbul, and I decided to purchase a postcard depicting the image to send to Harriet, my sister. I was just safely storing it in my bag when a booming voice, rather inappropriate in a holy place announced, 'Built by Roger the Second, they say, after his ship survived a terrible storm and he landed safely on the beach.'

I turned around and came face to face with Dottie who was standing a little closer than was necessary, particularly seeing as she was talking so loudly, indeed several people in the vicinity shushed. Unabashed she continued, 'I do think the outside looks more like a fortress than a church, though.'

Millie tactfully suggested that we move outside to allow others to view the mosaics, and I heard her add under her breath, 'in peace,' nevertheless Dottie allowed herself to be ushered outside, still extolling the feats of Roger in building the town around its small harbour.

Unfortunately, Millie now seemed to have been buttonholed by Dottie in search of a post office or *tabacchi* shop, and Joan was dogging Vanessa's footsteps again, and I did not feel inclined to try and attach myself to one of the couples (such as Paul and

Christine, or Tom and Angela). Never mind, I thought, I had booked this holiday alone, for me, and I would be independent and enjoy my own company, and so I set off to try and find the mediaeval laundry that Mary had suggested as another site of interest. Unfortunately, she had only provided us with vague directions, similar to those for finding the diorama in Taormina and so I dithered around a little to start with, trying to get my bearings.

I spied the beach first and wasted a few minutes watching a group of children playing happily on the golden sand under the bright blue sky. Then trying to remember the directions Mary had supplied, I walked down the narrow streets and as luck would have it, I found the ancient laundry opening tucked away on the left-hand side between two normal looking buildings.

The wash-house was built over a river and legend has it that its source was the tears of a nymph who had accidentally killed her lover.

I nipped down the stone steps and was gratified to discover I had the area with its rose-pink stone walls to myself and quickly snapped away at the basins and water spouts, which were carved as tiny lion heads. At one point, however I thought I heard footsteps coming down the stone steps but whoever it was hesitated and then retreated. Quickly I completed my photographs in the tiny area just in case other tourists decided to visit as it was a relatively cramped area, and I did not particularly want strange people in my pictures.

That done, I climbed back up to the main street and mooched around the shops. However, the blue sky of just a short time earlier had gone and was now covered in thick angry looking grey clouds. Suddenly the heavens opened in a downpour. One minute I was fumbling with the ties on my rucksack trying to retrieve my spare emergency plastic raincoat stashed away at the bottom, the next minute I was soaked to the skin.

My feet slopped about in my sandals. They had thick soles, comfortable for long walks, but which seemed to be sopping up the water like a sponge. I dithered, looking up and down the street trying to decide which was the quickest, easiest way back to the meeting point by the cathedral.

With the rain thundering down around me I did not hear the shout at first, and almost ignored it the second time, as I was not expecting to bump into anyone I knew, but as I looked around again in an effort to decide the way back to the cathedral I spotted a familiar figure hurrying towards me carrying a huge umbrella.

Normally I am not an umbrella person; I much prefer to wear a raincoat and a hat which thus leaves my hands free to carry any bags, but just at that moment I was not just wet, I was soaked through, in my thin summer clothes, and beginning to feel a little chilled. So Enzo with an umbrella, although unexpected (or was it? a little voice asked), was also very welcome, more so as I appeared to be lost and I hoped he knew the way to the church.

82

I felt a little self-conscious as I stood huddled next to him under his umbrella. I caught the faint whiff of cologne as he pulled me in close with an arm around my waist – firm but not too tight, a movement that brought back painful memories.

I had previously dated a local lad – briefly. I knew he had been keen on me for some time as he had marked me out for special attention when we had attended the same parties and discos. Eventually he wore away my defences and I agreed to go out with him. At first I found him pleasant enough company. He related some amusing tales, and although he had insisted on buying all the drinks he had not pushed alcohol on me or in any way attempted to take advantage. Until, that is, he came to walk me home, when he clamped an arm around my waist in a vice-like grip. As he was about a foot taller than me and rather muscular, being an amateur rugby player, I had almost been literally swept off my feet, but not in a good way. I could hardly move my arms, I felt hampered in walking and had difficulty breathing. His goodnight kiss had been none too gentle either. I did not agree to a second date.

The unpleasant recollection caused me to move slightly away from the Sicilian, but not too far as the rain was still falling in torrents and I wanted to remain under the umbrella's protection. Also I was aware that this was the first time I had been alone with Enzo and I felt a little uncomfortable; previously Millie and Joan had been with us. Even now, in the inclement weather there were few other souls abroad.

Skilfully he weaved our way through the narrow streets back to the cathedral. My sandals slopped and skidded on a cobbled area and I was grateful for his occasional steadying hand.

For a while we walked in silence save for the drumming of the rain on the umbrella and the splashes as we trod. Then, when it had eased a little, I turned to him and asked, 'Do you live here, Enzo?'

'Live here? In Cefalu?' Just for a moment I was transported back a few days to when I had bumped into him in Catania and we had had a similar conversation.

'In Sicily?'

'No, I live in Rome.'

We walked a little further and then I asked; 'So, are you on holiday as well?'

He gazed at me, for once seriously, and I realised my heart was thumping as I awaited his reply. What would it mean if he said no, that he was working? Working at what? Somehow I felt it was really important to discover if he was gainfully employed.

However, he caught hold of my arm and skilfully led me around the corner saying, 'We turn right just here. Mind that puddle. We're almost there now,' just as skilfully changing the subject, and thus avoiding answering my question. I considered repeating it, as possibly he had not heard it clearly in the inclement weather, but then, a little voice inside my head argued, he would have asked me what I had said. I remembered when we had chatted in the café in Catania he had asked all the questions but managed to evade the gentle probing of Millie and Joan, and consequently it was unlikely he would offer any personal information now.

Despite the rain I almost regretted it when we came in sight of the cathedral and I spied our group huddled together in an archway. Enzo withdrew his support and prepared to take his leave.

Since my unsuccessful attempt at questioning we had walked in silence. Aware of the rebuff I had been busy concentrating on where I placed my feet. Now as he turned away I asked him suddenly, 'Enzo, do you know Vanessa?'

He frowned and queried, 'Vanessa?'

'The woman who greeted you yesterday.'

'Ah,' he said, as recognition dawned. 'The woman who hugged me, you mean?' He grinned impishly and I felt myself flushing with embarrassment that he thought I might care, that I could be jealous. 'No, I have never met her before. But,' he added, nodding in the Sicilian manner of gesturing with the head, so that I turned to look behind me, 'I can see her now. She does not look so, how you say? Happy?'

Vanessa was not the only person who had noted our joint arrival. I was aware of a general murmur as people seemed to recognise him as the man whom she had greeted so enthusiastically yesterday and here he was, arriving now in my company. Millie appeared and nudged me playfully with her elbow.

'I said he was smitten,' she teased.

I have always mistrusted books where the dashing hero immediately falls in love with the narrator, as

Millie was suggesting, and thought that there had to be another reason for him to be associating with us, but as to what that was or why I could not imagine. I refused to believe that it was down to my dubious allure.

While Millie looked pleased with herself at her pronouncement and there was a general air of amusement that it was just a couple of days into the holiday and I was fraternising with the locals – or one particular local who had been seen being equally close with another woman yesterday – there was one person who definitely was not amused. I tried to avoid her gaze but I felt the daggers in my back and noted her eyes reduced to angry slits.

Millie was quite chatty on the bus driving onto out next hotel. Instead of sitting in her usual corner seat she had squeezed herself in between Richard and myself so she could have a good gossip. I let her prattle on, although I don't think I could have stopped her short of sitting somewhere else and I did not particularly want to sit with another person or inflict some of the others on her. She meant well, she was interested, nosy like most elderly ladies, but luckily not particularly hard of hearing so she did not raise her voice – which would have ensured that the whole bus heard.

However, her attention was soon diverted by the weather. The heavy rain had worsened and was now a torrential downpour. We were safely ensconced in the bus and were able to peer out the windows at people not so fortunate, hurrying along the pavements, as we drove into Palermo, the capital city of the island.

Here the traffic soon eased to a standstill as the roads were flooded; in places the cars were getting swamped and flumes rose from drains where their lids had broken under the pressure.

The next hotel was unfortunately a replacement. Normally I like to look up hotels online when booking a holiday so I know what to expect in general. While I am aware some people complain about anything and everything, I tend to look at the percentage of good to bad reviews and how recently the reviews have been left; after all hotels may change management and so reviews become irrelevant after a year or two.

I also like to look at the pictures; I avoid tours which stay in huge monumental skyscrapers, which unfortunately described the building we were pulling up beside. A monochrome grey, featureless monstrosity, its only adornment being a row of poles whose flags were being furiously buffeted by the wind.

Mary urged us to quickly depart the bus as we were blocking the road and to gather inside in the foyer, while porters hurriedly appeared to carry our cases inside.

I was pleased when allocated my room that despite the high-rise nature of the block that it was situated on level four, a manageable trek up the stairs. Once inside my room I looked around and was a little dismayed to discover that although I had paid a single supplement for this tour, which normally indicates a double room for sole occupancy, I had been allocated a tiny single room. However, it overlooked a side street and not the main road and so was relatively quiet, the only sound being the rain lashing on the windows and unfortunately, the sounds of the flags outside and their cords being whipped around by the wind and the fastenings clanging on the metal poles.

Once my case arrived I took a hot shower, quickly washed my hair so that I did not look too bedraggled and then alternated between drying my hair with the hairdryer and my sopping wet sandals. I also tried to dry them out using folded up wads of toilet paper to soak up the moisture and used the pressure of my feet as I stood up in them to do so, walking around the limited confines of my room to aid the process.

The dining room was situated on the lower ground floor and on my way there I bumped into Millie and Dottie hovering uncertainly around the bar on the ground floor. They wanted pre-dinner drinks but were having difficulty catching the eye of the barman who was slouched behind the bar reading a newspaper. I was reminded of my grandmother who rarely ventured into a public house and when she did she sat in the lounge bar; she had never sat in a public bar and never ventured in without my grandfather who always ordered their drinks.

'Can I help you ladies?' I asked loudly, hoping that

the man who should have uttered those words would hear. He did; he looked up, yawned, then turned his attention back to his newspaper, idly turning the page.

Dottie desired a gin and tonic and was trying to persuade Millie to indulge. However, Millie was not sure whether a dry sherry was too indulgent when there was nothing in particular to celebrate.

'Nonsense,' I told her. 'Every day is a sort of celebration when we are on holiday! Aren't you here to enjoy yourself?' To which she nodded agreement and decided perhaps a Cinzano and lemonade might hit the spot. Thus having reached a decision I stood as tall as I could and announced to the barman our drinks order, adding a red wine for myself. The barman had reached the sports pages of his newspaper and casually flicked through the last couple of sheets before folding it in half and stashing it under the counter, then reaching for a glass.

Our drinks in our hands, I supplied my room details for the tab and we moved aside to allow Vanessa and Joan to be served, the former who gave me a frosty look up and down as if contemplating whatever could Enzo see in me, a sentiment that I had also mulled over earlier while in the shower. Vanessa was taller than I, blonde and confident, what more could a Sicilian man ask for?

Dinner was a buffet affair and we found seats at the end of a long communal table and joined the queues at the serving dishes. Many of the dishes were empty and we hoped the staff would restock with fresh supplies. There were groups of younger people, who sounded possibly Eastern European, who not only failed to queue but knocked the elderly people to one side in their quest for food.

Afterwards, Millie and Dottie both tired after the long day and the hassle of the dining room retired to their respective rooms. Millie, who I had noted during our walk around Mount Etna, has some kind of skin condition covering her arms, had mentioned that the rain had not helped and she needed to apply some lotion, so there was enough time for it to soak into her skin before she slept.

'Otherwise I tend to stick to the sheets when I try and turn over,' she had commented with her customary grin.

Thinking of the prospect awaiting me of a tiny cubicle I wandered back to the bar a little hesitantly, ordered a second glass of wine and then settled myself in a corner with a newspaper that I had spied on a side table.

As it was an Italian newspaper I contented myself with flicking through the pages and gazing at the pictures. It was more a method to appear occupied and not a lonely, solo tourist than to avoid small talk with people I hardly knew and did not at this moment feel confident enough in joining their groups which were mostly comprised of couples, and butting into their conversations.

However, I was not alone for long. Angela, a mature lady of approximately retirement age approached me and pointing to a nearby chair asked if it was taken to which I shook my head and replied in the negative.

'Good,' she sighed. 'My feet are killing me and it is not as if we did an awful lot of walking today but my sandals are fairly new and they pinch.' As she spoke she surreptitiously slipped her feet out of her shoes and wiggled her toes.

'I know what you mean,' I sympathised. 'Getting them wet did not help. My sandals got absolutely soaked and I had a devil of job drying them out.'

We sat in companionable silence for a few moments and then she asked, 'You're here on your own aren't you? You're very brave.'

I considered this. 'Perhaps,' I conceded. 'But many people travel completely by themselves whereas I like to join a tour, to be taken places. So I am not really on my own. Besides I normally find that there are other people travelling by themselves, and everyone is very friendly.'

We looked towards the members of our group who remained gathered in the bar before relapsing into silence again, Angela rubbing her left foot and I returned to the newspaper.

'Speak Italian, do you?' she queried.

Again I smiled and shook my head. 'No, just looking at the pictures really,' I replied. 'With this storm raging outside it's impossible to go out for a stroll. I did not want to go up to my room to watch Italian TV or read a book, I can do that at home, but did not feel up to making small talk I'm afraid, so I gravitated to this corner.'

'Oh,' She paused before confiding, 'My husband speaks Italian. He's rather good actually. 'He speaks several languages. He travels a fair bit.'

'What does he do?' I felt compelled to ask.

Angela stared at me as if I had asked an impertinent question. 'Well, he is retired now, of course. We both are, so we can travel whenever we want to.'

I did not know what to say, as she appeared to evade my question. I thought she had implied he travelled with his occupation. I flipped over another page of the paper.

She seemed about to say something more but was forestalled by the appearance of her husband, Tom, who strode up with what looked like a glass of whisky in his hand, and I remembered that he was the man who had bought the hideous bottle of alcohol yesterday.

I was absentmindedly skimming through the newspaper as something to do, to keep my hands occupied if not my mind, when a picture caught my eye.

'Oh!' I uttered and felt myself flushing. I hoped that the corner in which I was seated had poor lighting and no-one had noticed. Unfortunately, someone had. Both Angela and her husband looked my way with almost identical expressions of interest on their faces.

'Something up?' Tom asked taking a step nearer.

Despite a desire to keep things private curiosity got the better of me. 'I'm not sure,' I admitted. 'I can't read Italian,' at which point I noticed the couple exchange glances that intimated they wondered what I was doing with an Italian newspaper. 'It's just, I thought I recognised someone in a picture.'

Tom carefully placed his whisky glass on a nearby table and then leaning over put a hand on the paper to aid his view.

'But it's just a superficial resemblance, really,' I added, hastily backtracking.

'Which photograph?' he queried. I pointed out a grainy print. All I had been able to make out was four men standing slightly proud of a crowd of people; two of the men appeared to be police, one of whom had his hand on the arm of a man who looked suspiciously like Enzo.

'Oh, it's just some burglar being taken for trial,' he said after a cursory glance at the article. Collecting his drink, he drained the glass before depositing it back on the table. 'Come along, Angela, it's getting late.

I bid them goodnight and then after they left and making sure no-one was looking I quickly tore the page out of the newspaper and stuffed it in my pocket. Then deciding to get rid of the evidence I took the paper with me into the ladies' toilets in the foyer where I hid it in the waste bin.

Chapter Six

Sightseeing in the Rain.

I lay in bed listening to the rain still beating on the windows, punctuated now and then by peals of thunder, and the occasional angry flash of lightening. Metal rings on the flags outside clanged against their metal poles as they were buffeted by a howling wind. Added to this, the room mini bar was an odd affair with a see-through door with a light inside that glowed like a night light.

This was not a particularly inspiring replacement hotel, although I could not blame the inclement weather on the establishment. Dinner had been an experience, with the crowds of people vying for the small amount of food, but at least my tiny narrow bed was comfortable, and I had succeeded in drying out my sandals so they would not be damp and uncomfortable to wear in future; although with the prospect of more rain tomorrow I proposed to wear my heavier shoes that I had worn for the trip up Etna previously.

My thoughts drifted around my head further chasing away any possibility of sleep. I was attracted to Enzo; I had been since the first time I had seen him riding his bike in Taormina – was he, as Millie declared, attracted to me? Was that why he seemed so attentive? But what other reason could there be?

On reflection of the picture, I realised I had not noted how old the newspaper was; I had just found it on the side and it could have been there for several days. Also, I had not noticed any names mentioned in the brief article on first perusal. Perhaps that was not Enzo's picture – he might have a twin brother or a cousin who looked remarkably similar – such things happen in books and films. Indeed, once whilst out shopping I had been stopped by a woman who was convinced I was an actress out of *Emmerdale*! Not normally a watcher of that programme the following evening I sat through an episode, but did not note even a slight resemblance to any of the cast.

With the continuing wind and rain outside, and the occasional rumble of thunder and flash of lightening highlighting the room sleep seemed unlikely.

I climbed out of bed and retrieved the scrap from my pocket and carefully tried to smooth it out. I rued again my lack of even a basic knowledge of the Italian language. The photograph might have been old or the article referring to a previous event of some unknown timescale; Tom had only given a merest outline that it involved a thief, a criminal. I checked again, this time more carefully; "Enzo" as a name was not mentioned in the piece, nor could I see any reference to "Lorenzo" its longer form. I recognised the place name of 'Palermo' and that was about all. Not really any the wiser I decided perhaps I had better try and get some rest.

Vanessa had been jealous of the attention he had shown today when escorting me to the cathedral. Enzo had avowed he had not met her before she had hugged him yesterday – did I believe him? Was Vanessa merely jealous or a woman scorned?

Was she a gangster's moll who might be out for revenge?

The rain from last night had eased but the sky was still overcast and gloomy as we drove into Monreale, an area just south of Palermo on Sicily's northern coast. In keeping with the weather our group was a little subdued as we joined the queue for entry into the cathedral through its rather fine bronze doors. Here we were greeted by our guide for this visit, a man whose youthful appearance and hesitant manner suggested that he was fairly new to the job, but his voice was pleasant and easy to listen to, even if he seemed at times a little unsure of his facts. Similar to the cathedral in Cefalu the interior boasted fine mosaics, again reminding me of those in Turkey.

Vanessa was back in annoying mode; when I was

trying to concentrate on the guide's talk of the cathedral she kept whispering to me that her camera was playing up again, and I wondered why she needed to fiddle with it just at that particular time. I took the earliest opportunity to lose her in the jostling crowd as soon as I could.

After lunch we headed into the heart of Palermo, the capital of the island since the ninth century when Sicily was under Arab rule, although the city is much older, having been founded by the Phoenicians in the first century AD, Mary informed us.

'The Norman Kings of Sicily chose the area for their hunting resort.' Across the aisle from me in the other corner back seat of the bus I spied Millie suddenly sit up and take notice of our leader's little talk. Then she positively wriggled in her seat when Mary added, 'A royal palace was built, although by our standards it was a rather modest affair,' at which point Millie slumped back down and turned to gaze out the window, her interest faded.

To begin this visit Mary gave us another brief guided tour. By now the sky had darkened and the threat of more rain seemed imminent. As we walked along we rustled ensconced in wet weather gear. I followed in the midst of the throng, feeling a little down, as after all I was on a summer holiday and that should have meant sun.

A short stroll down the corso Vittorio Emanuele lay the cathedral, which contains the tombs of many Sicilian kings and their wives, next to the royal palace. Millie nudged me in the ribs when Mary pointed this out. The cathedral is comprised of many architectural styles, although most of the Norman features were removed in mediaeval times, and much of the existing work is Gothic. The main entrance though still retains its fifteen century wooden doors. At one point the building was turned into a mosque after the Saracens had taken over the city in the ninth century. There still remains an inscription in Arabic from the Koran on a pillar outside; Sicily remains a multi-cultural society. I spotted Don busy taking snapshots while Cherie was making notes in a little book.

We then resumed our trek along the corso Vittorio Emanuele where approximately halfway along, marking the centre of the old city, is the Quatro Canti, or Four Corners (*'Four Candles?'* I heard someone query), a Baroque square from the seventeenth century, officially known as Piazza Vigliena. It is situated at the intersection of two main streets, the meeting point of four historic districts, with the streets and four baroque buildings making up its octagonal shape. Each building contains an ornate fountain rising to the height of the second floor with a statue of one of the four seasons, as well as a king and local saint in niches set into the third and fourth floors.

We passed several more churches, and some statues which apparently the locals did not much like in the Piazza Pretoria, hence its nickname of the Square of Shame, as behind iron railings and surrounding a central fountain stand sixteen stark white nude statues of nymphs, mermaids, humans and satyrs from the sixteenth century, that had been originally intended for Florence.

Our mini guided tour over, Mary handed out maps of the city centre highlighting possible sites to visit. I quickly turned my back on Vanessa as I glimpsed her chatting to Joan, and suggested to Millie that we might like to try and find the archaeological museum. Millie agreed, declaring that there was nothing else that she particularly wanted to see or do.

'Don't you want to see the Royal Palace?' I teased her; I felt sure that she would want to go back and view the Norman building.

Millie shook her head. 'After the discussion the other evening I rather suspect that it will be inundated with English tourists today,' she replied sounding a little jaded.

'But you enjoyed yourself tailing suspects around Aci Castello,' I pointed out trying to perk her up.

Millie hesitantly agreed but added, 'Until we discovered Richard was following us.' I admitted that had rather put a dampener on things and realised the embarrassment of the situation was the main reason for her present reluctance.

'This might be our final chance to check out a Norman castle,' I pointed out, 'a castle that could be the likely hiding place for the legendary sword of King Arthur.'

She tried one further objection: 'Legendary, meaning that it may not exist.'

'Do you want a boring holiday with the old fuddy-duddies who congregate around Mary, refused to climb Mount Etna and who have no imagination? I can leave you with Dilys and Mavis if you prefer?' I queried, naming the two eldest ladies in our group who insisted on sitting on the front seats of the bus ignoring the official seat rotation rule, who walked extremely slowly with the aid of sticks, often holding the group up, and went to their room as soon as the evening meal was concluded, never drinking so much as a small glass of wine to accompany it, and who glared at anyone who dared order a second glass; although having said that, I fervently hoped that I was still up to international travel which I reached their age, God willing.

Millie gave a little sheepish grin. 'Oh, all right then, the palace it is.'

I spied Vanessa bearing down on us so I swiftly pointed Millie down the street and we set off. It did not take us long to retrace our steps and soon we were standing in front of the building that had been the home to the Kings of Sicily; the oldest royal residence in Europe. I felt a little frisson of excitement, silly I know as there was no way that we would be able to find an object on an afternoon out for which people had been searching for hundreds of years. Millie and I exchanged grins.

'This is it!"

After their conquest of Sicily, a handful of years after they had invaded England, the Normans established Palermo as their capital and converted its original Arabian palace as the seat of their power. The Spanish also added later refurbishments in the seventeenth century.

We marvelled at the tiny chapel with its inlaid marble floor, intricately carved ceiling and mosaics retelling the biblical stories. We continued upstairs to the Royal Apartments, more recently decorated in the nineteenth century in velvet and gilt and then just as we stepped into the Salon of King Roger with its mosaics of peacocks and palm trees Millie hissed, 'Look! Look!'

I followed her gaze expecting to see something wonderful, and spotted Patrick and Hilary. Millie started frantically looking all around and a woman nearby attracted my attention and asked, 'Your friend, is she alright?' Although I was a little concerned I hastened to reassure her, claiming that she was just overcome by all the wonderful mosaics and other decorations, and drew my companion to one side.

'What are you doing?' I whispered.

'I'm looking for Richard.'

For a second my brain jumped back in time and I looked around expecting to see Richard the Lionheart, or his sword casually propped up in a corner. Then my mind caught up as common sense prevailed.

'He's bound to be here,' Millie added. 'I told you - this place will be overrun with English tourists.'

'It's just Patrick and Hilary,' I told her, but still gazing around out of habit. 'Two other people out of our whole group; there's nothing really sinister about it. This is the main site to visit in Palermo, and it was top of Mary's list of things to see.'

I could tell that Millie was not convinced and was more than a little paranoid that Richard was lurking somewhere behind us, watching our every move.

I put it down to a guilty conscience; we should never have spied on people ourselves in Aci Castello. I resolved in future to mind my own business as to what other people did on holiday, and try and persuade Millie to do likewise.

'Come on, I think we have seen all there is to see here, and as I mentioned before with all the other tourists about no-one is going to be poking and prying in corners trying to locate a missing sword,' I said. 'Plus with all the wall decorations and mosaics you would have to partly demolish the place first.'

Millie calmed down and agreed it was time we went in search of the museum otherwise we would not have enough time to look round its exhibits.

Once outside, I consulted the map to check we were going in the correct direction. However, it was not long before the rain that had threatened all morning started to fall steadily and soon we were wet and a little dispirited; Millie had even stopped singing, 'Do-do-do, little April showers,' every few minutes, for which I was grateful as it was beginning to grate on my nerves.

The maps Mary had given us proved to be rather inaccurate, only having the major roads named; little side streets and alleyways were missing and hence it was hard to follow. I sensed that Millie was beginning to doubt my map reading skills but I refused to be defeated.

'We need a man,' Millie announced.

'We do not,' I replied feeling a little insulted. 'I know exactly where we are.'

'We're lost,' she said. 'What we need is -'

'Some assistance ladies?'

It might have been that due to the rain that I had the hood of my jacket up and hence my hearing was a little muffled. Or it could have been the slightly croaky delivery that disguised his voice, whichever it was, I had not recognised it as being Enzo. Nor when I turned around did I immediately see his tanned, handsome smiling face. I saw a battered and bruised, cut visage, the cut lip raised one side in a sort of greeting. On further inspection I noted that he was standing slightly gingerly, favouring his left side.

'Ah, good, a man,' Millie said passing him her map, seeming to disregard his appearance in her relief at his, um appearance. 'We're trying to find the archaeological museum.'

Enzo looked down with a mixture of disbelief and disdain, after all as a local I assumed he knew his way around and did not need a map, otherwise why offer to be of assistance.

'Why?' he asked. 'It's closed.'

'Closed!' I could not believe it. How many times had I been on holiday and found various main attractions shut?

Enzo nodded, then grimaced. 'For renovation,' he

managed to say before his split lip started to bleed at which point Millie noticed his injuries. I was amazed she had not observed them sooner.

'Good heavens, what happened to you?' She began to fuss, producing a tissue which she attempted to use to dab at the blood until Enzo gently deflected her arm.

'A slight mishap,' he said. 'Nothing more.' He attempted to wave away his injuries with a Mediterranean shrug but the movement disturbed his precarious balance and had Millie fussing over him again. As if to prevent any more personal questions regarding his appearance he allowed Millie to take his arm and said, 'Actually the museum is quite close, just around the corner.'

I think in fact we turned three corners before that building came into view. And as Enzo had stated – it was closed for renovation. I cursed Mary and her list of possible things to do.

The rain started more heavily again. Millie complained that she thought her shoes were leaking and so Enzo suggested a coffee. I was beginning to suspect he spent most of his days hanging around coffee shops. Perhaps that was where Italian gangsters organised their crime – over coffee and a Danish, or whatever is the Italian equivalent. Cannoli, perhaps.

Although one look at his face revealed that beneath his tan he was pale and wan with dark circles, and not just actual bruises around his eyes. He looked strained, tired and in pain, as if it cost him a huge effort just to stand in the street and converse with us.

I refused to feel guilty, however. He had followed us, I assumed; or he had bumped into us in the street by sheer chance, which I thought unlikely. He had offered us assistance initially, not the other way around. And I was 100% sure that neither Millie nor I were responsible for his injuries.

But I did feel sympathetic enough to allow him to lead us to a little restaurant tucked away up a side street not too far away. I debated whether we walked at Millie's slow pace as her wet feet were beginning to throb or Enzo's injured shuffle.

The rain eased once more as we approached the bistro and both Enzo and Millie collapsed into the first available seats under the huge umbrellas. Enzo seemed to exhibit more than a passing acquaintance with the staff; a pretty waitress hurried over and joined Millie in attempting to administer to his wounds while a waiter hastily produced liquid refreshment, coffee – plus I suspected something a little stronger – to perk him up. With the girl, whom Enzo addressed as Cara Mia, which I initially took to be her name until the waiter called her Gina, pressing him for details, the story of how he came by his injuries unfolded.

My fevered brain was thinking Mafia or another run-in with the police – after all, despite the picture in the paper he was not in prison; either that was an old newspaper or the picture referred to a previous event, or possibly he was out on bail. I know nothing about legal procedures, either British or Italian, but he was obviously a free man and did not appear to be on the run. Nor, as his mobility appeared to be hampered, did he appear to be in hiding. In short he did not appear to be a man guilty of a crime – but then many such men, even after sentencing, profess their innocence: they are, they claim, misunderstood, purely a case of mistaken identity. I wondered again if indeed it was Enzo in the photo or perhaps a double, even possibly an (evil) twin brother.

Strangely, I did not doubt Tom's explanation or his rough translation of the article. As an Englishman I trusted him completely; Sicilians I viewed with a little more caution.

Enzo's story was sadly more mundane than my imaginings – he had simply skidded and fallen off his bike during all the rain last night. Nothing broken, he was quick to assure us – all of us, including Gina. It looked, he claimed, worse than it was, but somehow I doubted it.

While Enzo relayed the details about his accident Millie had been rummaging in her bag. I thought perhaps she was searching for medical supplies with which to ease his suffering. She placed several items on the table including a bottle wrapped in a scarf, 'The bottle leaks. I don't think it liked the flight over,' she whispered in an aside to me before diving back into her bag. Suddenly she clapped a hand to her head and declared loudly that she was a fool. All heads turned towards her.

'We passed the post office,' she cried. 'I forgot I

wanted to mail my postcards!' which pronouncement reminded me that I had yet to buy and write mine. Waving the offending articles in the air Millie jumped to her feet. Then she turned and started to march smartly up the street.

Enzo called across and said something to the waiter who nodded and hurried after her. When he caught up with the elderly woman, he gently put his arm around her shoulders and turned her around pointing her in the other direction. At a more sedate pace the unlikely duo set off once more towards their destination.

'She forgot the map,' grinned Enzo, waving the, by now, rather tatty piece of paper, which he passed back to me. 'A souvenir,' he said, 'of your holiday in Sicily.'

'I think I would like rather more than a soggy piece of paper,' I said.

'How about this?' and before I could reply he had wrapped his arm around my shoulders and kissed me lightly on the lips. All at once I felt a sudden glow spread from somewhere near my stomach and radiate out until I no longer felt cold and damp.

'Don't worry,' he said, kissing me again. 'Pepe is, I think, going to walk rather slowly with Millie.'

'But they are going to the post office?' I checked.

Another kiss, this time on my cheek. 'Of course, and they are now going along the correct road and not taking a detour,' he smiled and gave me a little squeeze. 'It's quite all right, the café is not busy in this weather, there is plenty of time.' He paused before adding, 'And so we are alone.'

Looking around I noticed a small girl siting at a nearby table with her mother and a friend who were drinking coffee while they chatted. I nudged Enzo and nodded in their direction. He gave a huge shrug, Mediterranean style, as if admitting defeat. Then he smiled and removed his arm. As I continued to look towards the small group he asked, 'She interests you, no? This small girl.'

The girl had a baby doll perched somewhat precariously on her chubby knees while she fed it from a large pretend milk bottle.

'Just remembering,' I replied a little regretfully over the lost years of my childhood, how the time flies. 'I used to have a doll just like that; for some reason I called her "Susan" and I spent hours feeding her with a similar bottle.'

'And why is Susan such an odd name for a doll?'

'Oh, I often used to call my dolls after whoever gave them to me or whichever aunt they reminded me of, but I don't remember having an Aunt Susan. Anyway,' I continued loath to reveal too many personal details or family secrets to this charming but essentially unknown man, 'I thought I really was feeding my doll milk from the bottle. It seemed to be some sort of magic. I would tip the bottle up to Susan's lips and little bubbles would appear as if she was actually drinking. Then one day the horrid little boy from next door trod on the bottle and cracked it. Turned out there was just a small amount of coloured water contained within an outer shell, comprised of two thin layers, and when you tipped the bottle up the liquid would flow up and collect in a reservoir making it appear that the doll was drinking her "milk" and then when the bottle was lowered it would then flow back down and recollect in the outer shell ready to feed her some more.' I paused and then added, 'You know, I think that might have marked a turning point in my childhood; after that I no longer accepted everything as being what they appeared to be.'

Enzo laughed. 'Sensible child.' Then he frowned and said, but more to himself, 'I wonder …' but what he thought was to remain a mystery as the mother and her friend paid their bill and, gathering the girl and her doll with them, they left.

'Ah, now we are alone,' Enzo said softly. He replaced his arm around my shoulders and gently pulled me closer.

I looked around. The waitress had disappeared into the kitchen and on such an inhospitable day anyone with any sense had stayed indoors.

With tentative fingers I traced the outline of the bruise down the side of his face, the graze along his chin and wiped away a smear of blood, as every time he smiled his split lip bled just a little.

'Does it hurt much?' I asked gazing into his clear brown eyes. Even his injuries could not disguise how handsome he was; what was he doing kissing someone like me I thought, when he could have someone tall and blonde and confident, like Vanessa?

He took my fingers and softly kissed the tips

before saying, 'No, not much.' Somehow I did not believe him and then a nagging voice in my head asked – what else has he said that I should not believe?

Enzo took us most of the way back to our rendezvous point with the rest of our group. For some reason (possibly Vanessa) he did not want to take us all the way but left us on the corner and watched, like a concerned parent, while Millie and I walked the last stretch along the pavement until we met up with the others. He gave no reason but hinted as to his injuries being the cause and flopped down on a nearby seat as if to say, "this is as far as I am going."

However, seated on the bus being taken back to the hotel we passed him hobbling up the street; there was a definite limp but he was managing just fine. I wondered again what sort of pick-me-up the waiter had given him.

I was not the only person who recognised him. I heard Angela tut and comment to her husband that my relationship with the young man did not bode well if he had been fighting, which made him sound like a hot-headed youth but all the same, I wondered whether he had lied to me. Again. This time over the cause of his injuries.

And was it just a coincidence his appearing, again, in Palermo? Millie might tease that he was smitten with me but if he *was* a professional burglar, was he after the sword as well? Although in his present condition I doubted he would make a very able burglar, unless of course he was faking or, at least, exaggerating the extent of his wounds; it might be possible to use make-up to mimic bruises but I would swear that the bleeding from his split lip was real. Had he already cased out the Royal Palace? Were his injuries due to a falling out among thieves?

Chapter Seven

One Night in Agrigento

After yesterday's bun fight feel to our evening meal and the resultant complaints we were treated to a sit down meal with complementary wine in a posh dining room, waited on by handsome men in smart suits. But not too much wine due to an early start the next morning on our way to Agrigento.

'Isn't that a song? By Tony Christie?' Richard asked, as Millie and I took our customary places on the back seat on either side of him. I was not sorry to be leaving Palermo, and hopefully the rain, behind.

We had left Palermo and were driving along the motorway when Mary became rather sombre. She pointed out that we were driving through the area where in 1992 a leading Sicilian magistrate, his wife and three members of his police escort had been killed in a bomb attack organised by the mafia. Even after almost twenty years the scars of the blast are still visible on the landscape. I shuddered as we silently passed the spot of the atrocity and shared a glance with Millie. I sincerely hoped that Enzo was not mixed up in such things.

We had several scheduled stops on the way to Agrigento; the hilltop town of Erice, Segesta with its temple and scenic Greek theatre, and Selinunte with, uh, more temples.

The cobbled streets of Erice, a wonderfully preserved mediaeval town, are pedestrianised. We had a brief guided tour and were then left to browse the (expensive tourist) gift shops and also find somewhere to eat a quick early lunch. Millie rubbed her hands with glee when Mary informed us that Erice had two castles, one dating from Saracen times and the other dating from Norman times. I, on the other hand, much as I love castles and old buildings in general, did not think I could face yet another morning spent searching buildings or tailing suspects, but I was glad to see that the older woman had recovered from her fit of embarrassment, or whatever it was, that had struck her in Palermo, and was now back to her old self, even if that meant an intention to spy on our fellow travellers.

Millie looked a little disappointed when I said we did not have time to view both, however she cheered up after I pointed out that if we did not have the time then neither would other members of our group.

She was further delighted when we discovered

that the Norman castle (which had been her preferred option, for obvious reasons) could easily be reached from the public gardens via a rather steep series of steps, to see the amazing views from its walkways and battlements. As most of our group trotted around 'oohing' and 'aahing' at the scenery Millie had one eye on the vista while the other was checking what the others were up to. Which was nothing suspicious; no-one darted around searching dark corners, and I could not decide whether she was upset or relieved that everyone was behaving like normal tourists.

I spent as much of the morning looking behind me as I did looking at the magnificent views in front – or what my feet were doing, and once Millie chided me that if I did not look where I was going I would come a cropper and end up with a battered face like Enzo.

I felt myself flushing. For some reason he was never far from my thoughts, however today he seemed too far from us in person as, try as I might, I could not spot his distinctive curly hair in the crowd. I felt a little deflated and abandoned despite any intention I might have had to keep him at arms' length thus deflecting any unwanted attention.

But was his attention unwanted? A little voice nagged. Hadn't I been a mite jealous when I thought he might be on friendly terms with Vanessa? And Gina the waitress?

I shook myself to get some sense into me, after all I had come on holiday to see the sites, immerse myself in some Sicilian culture and get some sun. Okay so far we had had plenty of rain, a thunder storm, and possibly the Sicilian culture I might be experiencing could be tied up with gangsters and that meant the Mafia – well what could be more authentically Sicilian than that?

I went native and had arancini for lunch; stuffed rice balls coated with breadcrumbs, deep fried and stuffed with ragù, mozzarella and peas. It was huge, about the size of my fist and delicious; one was enough.

After lunch we were on our way to our next visit and, despite my avowed intentions not to associate further with Enzo, I realised that I was missing him.

The theatre at Segusta is one of the most beautiful I think I have ever visited situated atop a (very) high hill. Although it must be a nightmare on a windy day, in the warm sun under a blue sky it seemed perfect; away from the noise and bustle of the modern towns, with more amazing views overlooking the countryside. I even forgot about Enzo for a while.

There is also one lone temple in the midst of the green valley, a curiosity in that it has no roof; that, and other features, suggest it was never finished. Nearby are the remains of the city, re-occupied in the Norman period and the reminder brought other thoughts, and I looked around once more for Enzo, and again was disappointed. Absence may make the heart grow fonder but I just felt a little frustrated. After his attentions previously, now I felt dropped like a hot brick. Should I have taken the hint when he had left us before the meeting point yesterday?

Our final stop was to admire the temples and Greek theatre at Selinunte, once a Greek colony. By this time Millie was a little tired and when she heard there was no Norman connection she was a little dispirited. She toured the main temple with Mary but declined to wander around those that were more derelict, being hardly more than a jumble of stones and hence a grazing ground for the local sheep and goats. Unfortunately, the physical exercise once more left my mind free to over exert itself.

By now I had stopped being frustrated and my mind was working overtime. Having been beaten previously – I refused to believe the story of him falling off his bike (he had been vague as to bicycle or motorbike) - as his injuries looked rather extensive, although Millie thought it perhaps appeared superficial bruising, hence it looked worse than it possibly was, I now thought he had been kidnapped, that other well-known mafia occupation, and was being held for ransom; by whom, why, or for what I had no idea.

When I mentioned this to Millie she merely tutted and muttered, 'Must be allergic to arancini.'

We had a little free time before dinner that evening and so Millie suggested we try and use the computer room to look for clues.

I asked her how we could find clues in a room we had not previously been in and she replied with a sympathetic look that suggested she thought the sun (or something else) had addled my brain, 'You know, use the computer to look up stuff, newspaper stories about Enzo and his "supposed" burglary skills -' even as she spoke I heard the quotation marks, '- or about Richard's travels in Sicily.'

I pointed out to her that neither of us spoke the language. She waved that obstacle away with a casual flick of her wrist. 'That shouldn't be a problem,' she declared. 'I heard Richard say he was going to use the computer before dinner and if we hang around after he has finished he might leave it set to "English language" for us.

'But what if he then decides to stay to see what we want to use the computer for?' I pointed out, a little surprised as I thought she had been trying to avoid Richard since her castle following exploits, but perhaps, I decided, sitting in close proximity to him on the bus every day had cured her of any feelings of embarrassment she had momentarily suffered.

'Then I will just email my sister,' she declared.

'Well, we can do that anyway,' I said, 'Let her know you're well and enjoying yourself. You are enjoying yourself?' I peered at her, hoping for an answer in the affirmative.

'Oh yes, this trip has been such fun! Trailing suspects round old castles, meeting handsome young men.' She giggled. 'I have already sent my sister a postcard, posted it yesterday in Palermo; she has not got a computer.' I stared at her. 'But Richard doesn't know that,' she added.

As this hotel in Agrigento did not seem to supply complimentary newspapers in its small reception area I agreed that we might as well give it a go. We hovered in the doorway of the tiny computer cubicle while Richard plodded away with one finger, finally he looked up, said, 'Almost done,' and with a flourish of strokes using the first fingers of both hands he then sat back and surveyed the screen with satisfaction. 'All yours, ladies,' he said as he stood up. 'I've left it logged in but if you have any difficulties here's the password,' and he pointed out a scrap of paper on the table. 'I've left it in English for you as well. Enjoy.' And he left the room backwards, giving us a mock little bow as he went.

Millie presented me with the chair. 'There you go,' she said.

For a few seconds I gazed at the blank screen. Then retrieved the scrap of now rather crumpled newspaper and placed it on the desk. I noted the name of the paper and entered it into the search field and pressed enter. Hesitantly I brought up details for today's edition of the paper and then slowly scrolled down its front page, Millie peering over my shoulder. Although the computer had been set to English the newspaper in front of us remained in its original Italian form. As far as I could tell there was nothing that suggested there was a continuation of the article.

Next I entered the heading at the top of the piece of paper but all that brought up was the feature I had torn out previously.

I turned to Millie. 'Well I cannot think of anything

else. I don't know how to bring up old copies of the paper, so without knowing what it was actually about I am stumped. So what Arthur bits do you want to look at?'

Millie suggested entering 'King Arthur and Sicily.' This brought up several items including something that looked promising in Agrigento, our current location. Millie giggled and nervously I clicked the link naïvely thinking we might be uncovering information hitherto unknown to the rest of our group, but our enthusiasm waned when "The King Arthur" turned out to be the name of a luxurious hotel located somewhere nearby. We looked at its details anyway.

'Shame we are not staying there,' Millie commented. 'It looks very nice.'

Next, I changed "Arthur" to "Richard" and we did manage to discover a little more information, however browsing other websites. The French were also briefly involved in the scuffles as allies of the English it seemed, and Richard attacked Messina before staying there for the winter, Sicilian winters being milder than British ones. Richard's sister was released from imprisonment, and her dowry, or according to some sources her inheritance following her husband's death, was returned. Richard also proclaimed his young nephew, Arthur, as his heir and Tancred promised the hand of one of his daughters in marriage when the boy came of age, Arthur, as noted previously only being four years; we still did not know the age of his prospective bride, not that it was important but I was just curious.

Satisfied, Richard left for the Holy Land giving his new friend, Tancred, his sword, Excalibur as a gift. Whether Tancred believed it to be the real Excalibur is not known but he accepted the gift.

'Perhaps he did not want the embarrassment of looking a fool if he later claimed the sword was not genuine,' Millie suggested.

I considered this but thought that wars and foreign invasions had been started for other petty reasons, but perhaps fighting the Crusades at this time was enough. 'Anyway, if he was given a replacement sword it must have been of a good enough quality to satisfy him,' I suggested.

However, when Tancred's treasury was looted by King Henry IV of the Holy Roman Empire who was also the King of Germany and later became King of Sicily, the sword was not there. There was also a link in that Henry was married to Tancred's aunt; furthermore, he received Richard the Lionheart as a prisoner from Leopold of Austria after Richard had been captured on his way back from the Crusades, and demanded a huge ransom for his release.

After a while it seemed like we were going round in circles reading the same information just presented slightly differently. I looked at my watch and decided I was hungry. Millie agreed there was just time for a pre-dinner drink in the bar to commiserate ourselves on our lack of success; we were no further in discovering if Excalibur had ever been found in Sicily or the whereabouts of a likely location, other than it had last been seen in Tancred's treasury, which we still had no concrete evidence as to whether that was in the Royal Palace in Palermo, or some other location. I discounted Millie's suggestion of Messina on the basis that Richard had stayed there over winter, as he had subsequently given the sword to Tancred on his departure, but as I told Millie, it was highly unlikely we would uncover any new information so easily, as if it was there for anyone to see on the internet doubtless other people would have seen it and discovered the sword before now.

Likewise, I had failed to discover any further details regarding Enzo's possible criminal past – or present, if he was also after the sword. It was foremost on my mind that I had not seen Enzo today. His injuries might have flared up or he could have encountered more crooks. Or he could still be in Palermo searching the Royal Palace.

We did bring up one interesting item in our quest, which left both Millie and I momentarily speechless and at a loss. Stunned, I had logged out the computer and we were halfway down the corridor on our way to dinner when a thought occurred to me. 'Damn!' I muttered.

Millie looked at me in concern. 'What is it?'

'You know what we – I- should have done?' She looked blankly me and I realised computers where not an area of her expertise or familiarity despite it being her suggestion. 'I should have used the translation bit to translate the newspaper clipping.' She still looked blank so I explained further as I turned around to go back. 'I could log back in using the password Richard left, then in google use a translate Italian to English feature, cut and paste the Italian words of the newspaper article into it and it would translate the piece into English for us. It could take a while though and I am hungry.' As I paused a French couple passed us on the way to the computer room. 'Well, that's that then.' I said, 'Decision made; we eat. Maybe we can see if the computer is free and have another go later.'

That evening despite my best efforts to sit with people I had so far not socialised with, Millie had saved me a seat next to her, after I had been delayed briefly in the bar by Richard checking we had managed our computer endeavours satisfactorily. Also on the table, however were Tom and Angela, and Vanessa and Joan. Still, at least I did not have to sit with Richard and put up with more of his dodgy inuendoes; Millie and I suffered enough with these on the bus.

Everything went smoothly until Angela brought up the subject of Italian men, or rather Sicilian men, or Enzo to be precise. She had noticed his presence, or rather lack of presence today. As with certain other women in our party (and possibly one or two of the men) when he had popped up previously she had been aware of his tanned good looks and easy going Mediterranean charm and despite the scenic delights of Erice and Segusta and the cultural allure of

Selinunte she had noted something, or someone was missing.

'Tell me, Carrie,' she said as soon as she had finished her soup. 'What happened to your friend?'

I took this to mean she had spotted him yesterday battered and bruised and perhaps thought me responsible and I dribbled the last remnants of my appetiser and narrowly avoided splattering it down the front of my top. I felt all eyes on me and I was unsure whether this was due to Angela's question or my eating mishap.

'That local man you seemed to have picked up,' she continued thus allowing me time to compose myself. 'The one with the curly hair; I don't remember seeing him today.'

'I expect he had to work,' I answered, a little lamely.

'Oh, I thought the way he swanned around the tourist sites that perhaps he was on holiday as well,' she paused before adding "a busman's holiday" perhaps?'

There was some whispering between Joan and Vanessa and I gathered that they were trying to decide what this meant.

I was saved from answering as at that moment the waitress appeared and started removing our plates. However, it was only a momentary respite.

'Which local man is this?' Tom enquired.

'You must have seen him,' his wife replied, straightening out the cutlery in front of her in readiness for the main course. 'He appeared with a bicycle when we first arrived, Catania I think, no Taormina, and then I am sure I spotted him up Mount Etna in motorcycle leathers. Quite becoming really. And then of course, we all spotted him when Vanessa,' she glanced across towards that lady, 'hugged him and greeted him as if for all the world he was a long lost friend, but he seemed,' and here her eyes, which I noted were a pale, cold bluey-green turned briefly to stare at me, 'to be a special friend of Carrie's.'

'Not a special friend,' I hastened to correct her, surprised that she had taken notice of him, especially when I had only glimpsed him briefly in Taormina and I thought at Mount Etna that she and her husband had been too engrossed in buying the hideous bottle of wine to notice anyone else; obviously it wasn't just me struck by his dashing good looks. I did not think she had taken an interest in the newspaper article I had shown them. 'Just someone I met - we met, Millie and I.' I turned to my older companion for some support but she was deep in conversation with the waiter over how much pasta she wanted.

I became aware that Angela's were not the only cold eyes around the table as Vanessa's brighter blue ones glittered fiercely.

I allowed the waiter to heap some pasta on my plate with some sort or sauce, the nature of the conversation wiping the details of our proposed menu from my mind.

'Tall chap?' Tom queried.

'Not particularly,' Angela replied, 'but rather striking. He has rather thick curly hair but the odd thing is, it is quite grey. 'You know, a lot of men these days dye their hair as much as the women–'

'Oh! And pluck their eyebrows!' Millie exclaimed. 'I cannot abide a man with plucked eyebrows!'

'You would prefer them all to be hairy, would you?' Vanessa asked. 'The sort with little tuffs that stick up.' She raised her hands to her face demonstrating huge tufted brows.

'No,' the older woman replied decisively, 'a little neatness is all very well in its place, but some men just seem to overdo it. It just makes them look effeminate.'

'Perhaps you mean androgynous?' Vanessa queried.

'I know what I mean,' stated Millie a little primly as she proceeded to try and eat her pasta delicately.

Tom, expertly twisting his fork to create an immaculate spiral of spaghetti popped it into his mouth, chewed, then said, 'Grey haired huh? But a youngish chap?'

'Yes, that's the one,' Angela confirmed. 'Once you have seen him you cannot mistake him.'

'No, quite,' muttered Tom and I was glad to be left out of the conversational loop for a while and was able to concentrate on eating. After a narrow squeak with the soup I did not want to flick sauce everywhere.

However, while the couple continued to discuss the merits of Enzo, Vanessa leant towards me and

125

whispered, 'Well, you're a dark horse, aren't you?'

I turned and stared at her.

'It seems everyone knows you have bagged yourself an Italian stallion.'

I hoped not. Or rather, I was not sure whether I hoped not. I did not want other people to know my private concerns. Suddenly, I seemed to lose my appetite. Then Tom stated, 'Yes, he seemed vaguely familiar, but some people are like that -,' I dropped my fork onto the floor, '- you feel sure you have met them some place before whereas in fact you haven't, just someone who looks a bit like them. But,' he stared into space in front of him, as if attempting to conjure Enzo up in person, 'perhaps it was him, after all,' he said thoughtfully.

I hoped he was not referring to the article in the newspaper that he had sort of translated for me the other evening. I made a mental note to check for a recent paper in our next hotel to see if it was indeed a current news item, although how I could tell if there were no pictures I had no idea. I could hardly scan every page for the name "Enzo" – I had no idea, I realised what his surname was. I needed to recheck the clipping again, I decided, for any identifiable names, not just his, in an effort to identify the other men in the picture, as well as an aid to discovering what the article was about.

I bent down to retrieve my fork just as Millie decided to move her leg and inadvertently sent it skidding across the room, where a rather surprised waiter quickly scooped it up.

'So, tell us,' Vanessa prompted with a hard edge to her voice, 'what sort of work does *your friend* do?'

'I don't know,' I admitted, a little flustered by all this attention. 'He's not really a friend, more of an acquaintance really.' I looked to Millie for support, after all she had selected this table and our dining companions, however she was busy concentrating on her food and seemed oblivious to the conversation. Perhaps I thought, she is a little deaf after all; I had noted her on occasions talking slightly unnecessarily loud as people hard of hearing tend to so. Perhaps I am sitting on her poor side for hearing.

'Hmm, not much of a *friend*,' agreed Vanessa disdainfully. I recalled her seemingly friendly overtures when we first met; they had not lasted long.

I hoped the conversation would move onto a new topic. I decided to give it a nudge.

'Where are we off to tomorrow? Is it more temples?' and even to my ears I sounded artificially bright.

'Yes, the Valley of the Seven Temples, although I do believe that there are actually ten of them,' Angela replied. 'More importantly, I had a quick word with Mary and we should get some good weather tomorrow.'

'Oh, that's good, darling, if we are going to be out in the open all day,' said her husband.

'Well, not all day, darling,' Angela retorted. 'We're due to see the villa in the afternoon with all the mosaics; that'll be inside.'

I finally managed to finish my mound of pasta

with the use of my dessert fork to replace the one that I had lost.

After dinner Millie and I managed to evade Dottie who we spotted approaching us across the bar with the air of someone with something they intend to discuss. We swiftly nipped around a corner and sped up the corridor as fast as we could having just indulged in piles of pasta followed by pudding, reminiscent of our recent endeavours in Aci Castello, and made our way back to the computer room unhindered, only to discover the room had been locked for the night.

I rued again my failure in using a translate facility earlier. Was it because deep down I feared Enzo was a crook but my subconscious was stopping me from being able to confirm it?

Chapter Eight

Having a Smashing Time

I awoke to blue sky and, for some reason despite the sun and the promise of a fine day, felt a little disheartened. I was unsure whether it was due to a feeling of having been abandoned by Enzo yesterday, that he had lost interest in me, or whether it was down to my resolve, that even though I admitted I was attracted to him, no good could come of the association and I should be pleased that he seemed to have desisted in his attentions. I resolved, yet again, to give my full attention to the remainder of my holiday.

The Valley of the Seven Temples are not in a valley, we discovered, but strewn across a high hill top, not far from Agrigento, and as Tom had pointed out last night, being so exposed it was good to have fine weather. The temples are in varying states of decay, ranging from some in an almost complete condition as the day they were erected, to the last remaining ones (mainly those which we had to cross the road to reach), that were little more than a pile of stones amongst some trees and possibly were still awaiting full investigation; presumably that was why they did not appear to count in the titular "seven" almost as if tacked on as an afterthought.

Our guide, thankfully just for the morning, was fervent in her endeavour to impart her information. She shouted in a loud shrill voice that became more irritating as the day progressed and in order to pack in as much technical information as possible she spoke at an incredible speed, sometimes tripping over her words in her keenness to display her vast mass of knowledge. Whilst I was content to know they were the finest Greek temples to be found outside of mainland Greece, constructed of the Doric variety during the fifth and sixth centuries BC, my own enthusiasm waned, as at each edifice she would proclaim its dimensions in detail and by about the third temple I found I did not particularly care about the size of the columns in relation to its height, or how many grooves or steps there were.

Gradually our little group spread out, not just to appreciate the sites but to edge away from her fervour, as if it was contagious. However, her voice carried quite a distance and it seemed impossible to escape. I felt a little sorry for Mary as she struggled to keep us all together but having gathered the stragglers back into the fold, whenever we paused to view a temple and the guide opened her mouth, people suddenly discovered a need to wander off again.

While there were at times during our morning walk crowds of other tourists, it was nothing to the throng that wended its way around the villa Piazza Armerina complex which we viewed after an early lunch. We trudged more or less in single file to peer over shoulders and the protective railings at the amazing array of decorative mosaics. Even the entrance pathway was a mosaic although admittedly a plainer one than had originally been designed as a walkway, even so, we trod warily in deference to its antiquity.

We had to strain to hear our guide, Davide, above the noise of the workmen constructing the protective building over the mosaics, as well as the murmur of the crowds and the voices of the other guides, although as is usually the case, these professionals attempted to take it in turns to view the exhibits and explain them to their groups.

Unfortunately, for me, my resolve to have nothing more to do with Enzo should he appear, waivered as soon as I saw him chatting with the security guard at the entrance as if they were old friends. He still looked battered and bruised but the scabs and grazes showed signs of healing and he looked brighter as he smiled at me as I drew closer.

'Ah *cara mia*, I wondered what time you would get here! I was sure you were bound to visit,' he announced, beaming and attempting to lean forward and plant a kiss on my cheek. I felt everyone was staring at us, especially as last night over dinner Enzo had seemed to be the main topic of conversation, and feeling embarrassed I quickly turned my head and his kiss landed on my ear. He took a step back. 'You are not pleased to see me?' he asked frowning.

No, I thought, remembering how he had similarly greeted the waitress and I had since discovered what it meant. However, he proceeded to tag along beside me throughout our visit, much to my embarrassment until I felt that I and Enzo were also on display, as my fellow travellers stared at us, a couple of the older ladies nudging each other and pointing, as much as they were looking at the mosaics. There might have been an element of fun in their some of their joking and leg pulling but I feared our association might be the topic of conversation at dinner again tonight.

How could Enzo do this to me? After previously he had seemed to want to distance himself from the group.

Our group had discussed the proposed visit to the Villa Romana del Casale over breakfast and I had caused more than one eyebrow to raise when I had queried, 'Isn't that the villa with the famous mosaics of the women wearing leather bikinis?' The laughter had eventually died down but as no-one else seemed to have heard of these woman I had begun to doubt myself, but sure enough we came to a room were several women athletes were wearing what looked remarkably like bikinis as they competed in various sports such as running or discus throwing, with one woman in the centre wearing a victor's crown and carrying a winner's palm. I smiled to myself as various people gazed in awe at the pictures and then turned to me and commented, 'You were right; they are wearing bikini's!' I felt myself relax and begin to enjoy the visit.

The villa is vast, crammed with many wonderful mosaics of extraordinary naturalism and vitality. Ensnared in the throng, we traversed through the aisles sometimes at a snail's pace, although that was no hardship with such fine art on display, and all the time Enzo was at my elbow, occasionally pointing out what our guide was explaining, and although I appreciated his helpfulness I could not help feeling that his constant attention was an attempt to make up for the lack of his presence yesterday.

When I queried this, he informed me that his injuries had begun to ache a little and knowing Erice and Segusta were hill top destinations he had decided to rest up. I felt again that little twinge of alarm that he knew our destinations. It was one thing to have an admirer, another to feel that I was being stalked.

'Ah, but all tourists visit Erice and all the Greek temple areas,' he had exclaimed when I quizzed him about this. 'The same as all groups visit the mosaics.' Yes, I wanted to say, but not all visit on the same days – how did he know that we were going to Erice yesterday and not today? Where did he get his inside information?

Millie was eager for me to divulge all, as she expressed it as we sat side by side on the bus later that afternoon. She refused to be diverted by discussion of the possible dinner menu – 'there will be some sort of pasta or fish; or fish with pasta' – she pronounced and as we sat huddled in one corner of the back seat, with Richard in his customary position in the middle, she verbally poked and prodded me with more dexterity than my office colleague, Pat.

Of course, she tried to be subtle about it; wasn't he handsome? Such dashing good looks; but then aren't most Italians? It's that warm Mediterranean sun giving them the embodiment of healthy good looks. Thinking she had softened me up she then edged a little closer and asked if he had said what he was doing at the villa?

'I thought that was obvious,' I replied a little sharply. 'He was following us, well me, around.'

'Ah!,' she said archly, but was he just at the villa? Had he been elsewhere in town?'

'I don't know! He does not tell me his every movement.'

'Well, I think you are playing this all wrong, Carrie,' she chided me. 'You missed a chance to find out what he is up to.'

'So, you admit it, do you? That he must be up to something and not associating with me because he likes me?' I felt a little offended

Millie thought about this and then said, 'Well I am sure that he likes you, Carrie, I've said that all along, but well,' she hesitated, glancing across at Richard who seemed to have fallen asleep with the movement of the coach; his head had drooped to one side and nodded along with the vehicles' movement. 'According to my guidebook the nearby town has several Norman churches and the city of Piazza Armina has a large Baroque Norman cathedral. While we were at the Greek temples this morning he might have been doing a bit of sightseeing of his own. I mean, here he is again.'

I smiled at her, pointing out that these may be Norman constructions but were churches and not castles, and that the probable constant presence of clergy would have prevented these buildings being used as hiding places, besides which there was the danger that some abbot or priest might find the sword, I informed her, and proclaim it some sort of holy relic.

She meant well but somehow I could not take it all seriously; I mean it was all very well to talk in the bar of an evening after a glass or two of wine about King Richard the Lionheart giving the legendary sword of an equally legendary ancient British King to a Sicilian king, and it had been fun following various people around Aci Castello, but when you stopped and thought about it, it did seem rather farfetched that after all this time people were still searching for Excalibur in Sicily.

'I think you have Normans on the brain,' I told her, 'and possibly a touch of the sun. Just because legend has it that the sword is hidden in a Norman castle it does not mean you should try and ransack every mediaeval building we pass, and I don't know why Enzo was here this afternoon, perhaps he likes mosaics, maybe he has family in the area, and no -' I said as I realised I might have used the wrong word,

'I don't mean "family" as in gangsters, I mean a cousin or something. After all he was chatting to the staff when we arrived.'

Millie sat back and folded her arms across her chest a little petulantly.

'And,' I reminded her, 'you've forgotten what we discovered on the computer last night.' I leaned in a little closer to her and whispered, just in case Richard was only pretending to be dozing. 'The sword was found in England in the nineteenth century.'

'And promptly lost again,' she reminded me. 'It could be anywhere.'

I suspected she would continue looking for Norman architecture.

We arrived back at the outskirts of Catania late afternoon and after booking into our sea front hotel I debated whether to go for a swim or head to the shops. I still had gifts to buy and the end of the trip was looming, and although I had booked for the extension on Vulcano Island, I suspected that as often happens in small island locations, any such shops would sell select merchandise at inflated prices. Guilt over being distracted by a certain person (and I did not mean either Arthur or Richard) and not remembering my friends and family before now won and I set off to browse a small row of shops and road side stalls I had noticed as we passed by in the coach.

I had not gone far before I realised I had picked up a shadow. I turned around quickly suspecting a pickpocket or some other unsavoury character attempting to catch me unawares but I might have guessed. Enzo.

He gave me a lopsided grin, then touched the healing scab on his lip as if to remind me he was wounded. Well, he might have been injured but I was feeling more than a little irritated by his constant pursuing. Some women might have been flattered, I guess, but I have never been the type to attract admirers in this fashion. Yes, he was handsome. Yes, he could be good company, but just at the moment I needed to concentrate on shopping for gifts.

'So what are you going to buy, *cara mia*?' he asked me slipping an arm around my waist.

'Don't call me that,' I objected, wriggling free. 'My name is Carrie.'

He stopped for a second. 'I apologise, Carrie," he said momentarily serious. 'So, what are you going to buy?' and after a moment's pause he added, 'and why are you angry with me?'

'I don't know what I am going to buy,' I said crossly. 'I need to look.' I had stopped when he had paused, now I started towards the shops once more. 'And I am not angry with you.' He caught up with me and I glanced across at him. 'I'm not,' I repeated. 'Well, perhaps, just a little irritated. You just keep cropping up!'

After a pause I realised he did not understand the word as he repeated it softly, 'Cropping up?'

'Appearing,' I explained. 'I am trying to have a holiday and you keep showing up wherever I am.

How do you do it?' I asked. 'How do you know where I am going to be?'

'Magic!' he grinned.

'No, I am serious,' I said. 'It is beginning to get a little creepy.'

He stopped in his tracks again, and repeated, 'Creepy!' but this time I knew he knew what it meant. 'I thought you liked me,' he said a little wistfully.

'I did, I do, but,' I hesitated, thinking how to explain things. 'I'm not the sort of person who has a quick holiday affair,' I said. 'I don't know you.'

'Then get to know me!' He grinned once more and took a step towards me, his hand outstretched towards my waist.

'I need to go shopping,' I insisted, evading his embrace once more with a swift side step.

'Then let's go shopping!' he announced and gripping my hand he led the way towards the row of shops.

However, the uneasiness continued. Once inside the nearest gift shop I found it hard to browse as Enzo kept pointing out items saying, 'How about this? Or this?' items that were either hideous or expensive or just plain hideously expensive. I could not concentrate on perusing all the bric-a-brac on display, trying to think what my sister or my nephew might like.

'This, now you must buy one of these!' Enzo insisted presenting me with a rock encrusted bottle of something.

'No,' I said tersely.

Undeterred he presented me with another bottle. 'Here, red wine. Everybody loves red wine.'

I did not know what to say, so I just glared at him.

'Ah! This is the one.' He touched my arm lightly to attract my attention.

I looked down at his hand and he quickly withdrew it but still continued to hold the bottle up for my consideration. The label showed Venus, goddess of love, arising naked from her seashell, her long hair flowing over her shoulder, partly covering her body, her hands gripping something like a towel around her thighs. It looked slightly less ghastly than the other similar bottles I had seen. Possibly Pat, my friend back in the office might like it, and on closer inspection surprisingly it did not seem much more expensive than a regular bottle of red wine.

'You're sure this is drinkable and not just for show?' I asked. Enzo frowned as if not quite understanding the question. 'I assume this has not been in the shop for years and will taste like paint stripper.'

'No, no,' he hastened to assure me. 'This is good wine.'

I cast another glance over the selection of bottles on offer but it appeared to be the only one of this type, with a picture of Venus on the label, and covered in a slightly more tasteful arrangement of lava chippings.

I selected a tea towel portraying a map of the island for my sister Harriet together with a small bottle of limoncello, the Italian lemon flavoured liqueur – although not a rock encrusted version.

After I had paid Enzo, insisted that he would assist me further in carrying the bottle of wine. Now that I had bought some gifts I felt a little more relaxed and did not mind when Enzo slipped his arm around my waist. His touch was firm but not restrictive.

As I walked alongside Enzo, his stride matched to mine with only a hint of the limp remaining from his injuries, it brought to mind once again the previous unpleasant experience with the rugby playing young man who had walked me home in a vice-like grip as if to assert his mastery over me.

Just as a test I wriggled a little further out of Enzo's grasp and he obligingly loosened his hold slightly. I felt myself smiling; I did not feel trapped, I could move, I could breath. I felt perhaps I could get to like Enzo. I could –

The bottle smashed into several pieces; jagged fragments of glass scattered everywhere. Red wine splashed up my legs.

I looked down aghast and then transferred my gaze to Enzo. He was standing stock-still staring at the debris at his feet, a frown marring his features, as if he had never seen a bottle break into bits before.

'Oh! *Cara mia*! I am sorry,' he cried. He bent down and started to look over the pieces, gingerly lifting up some of the bigger fragments of glass.

I bit my tongue; I wanted to remind him again, that it was close, but that was not my name, but somehow I did not think that this was the time.

'That was the only bottle like it, as well,' I said regretfully. The others in the shop were too tacky

140

even for Pat. 'There's a bottle bank over there,' I pointed across the road. 'We can put as much of the glass, the larger pieces, in there to ensure that no-one, a child, cuts themselves."

Enzo was still sifting through the remnants as if searching for something but there was nothing salvageable except the soggy label which dangled limply from his fingers.

'Enzo,' I repeated. 'There is a bottle bank across the road.'

Somehow we managed to scoop up most of the glass and dump it in the bin. Enzo still clung onto the label and when I suggested he throw it in the rubbish bin he said he would keep hold of it and look around for a replacement bottle for me. He was sure he had seen a similar one somewhere.

'Etna?' I suggested with a smile, teasing that he might have to travel back there to find one, not that it was a huge distance, Sicily being an island, but he remained thoughtful and the joke went over his head.

'Here,' he thrust some notes into my hands. 'In case I don't find another bottle.'

'It was an accident, Enzo,' I said. 'Don't worry about it.' I looked down at the wad of notes. This was much more than the bottle had cost. 'Enzo, take this back,' I insisted trying to hand the money back. 'It was an accident.' I repeated but even as I said it a little scene replayed itself in my head ending with Enzo knocking the bottle against the sea wall. 'Wasn't it? Enzo?'

He stood silently in front of me.

'I'm sorry, Carrie,' was all he could say.

I reached forward and stuffed the money in the top pocket of his shirt.

'Well, sorry doesn't cut it,' I said acidly. 'Why would you want to do something like that? Convince me to buy the damn thing and then deliberately break it! Why? Why Enzo?'

He gave one of those expressive European shrugs.

'Huh! Men!' I said. 'You..!' I clamped my mouth shut; for a moment words failed me. 'Don't ever speak to me again! Don't follow me, don't stop me or anything! I'll find my own replacement bottle, thank you very much!' And with that I turned on my heel and marched away trying not to swing the bag that contained the bottle of limoncello.

Chapter Nine

Lost

When I reached the hotel I hastened up to my room to be alone. I could feel the tears welling up and I did not want to cry in public, not with Vanessa and her shadow, Joan, in the foyer watching me hurry up the stairs.

Sometimes even a relaxing holiday can have its stressful moments although why I should cry over a bottle of cheap wine I did not know.

A knock on the door heralded the arrival of Millie enquiring if I wanted a pre-dinner drink in the bar. She stood hesitantly on the threshold then invited herself into my room.

'Is everything alright, Carrie?' she asked, concern etched across her kindly elderly face.

I told her about the incident with the bottle.

'Maybe it was an accident,' she tried to reassure me. 'Perhaps he tripped and put his hand out to stop himself from falling, forgetting he held the bottle.

What was in his other hand?' she asked innocently.

I gave a weak little smile but refrained from replying – me. Enzo's other arm had been around my waist.

Syracuse, our local guide for the following morning informed us, was once a major power in ancient times before Palermo became Sicily's capitol. It was the birthplace of Archimedes, the engineer and mathematician who discovered *pi* and other things to do with circles and spheres. He also discovered the weight displacement principle during his Eureka moment whilst taking a bath. He was killed during the siege of Syracuse and his tomb is reported to be somewhere in the area but no-one knows exactly where. I felt haunted by prominent ancient personages with lost tombs.

Our first visit of the day was to the Greek amphitheatre. Built into the slope of the hillside, it was once one of the largest in antiquity seating many thousands of spectators. It is still used today during the summer months even though the seats are chipped and some of the narrow steps are missing stones and thus difficult to traverse. I noticed Vanessa holding tightly onto the arm of our young male guide supplied to give local knowledge to supplement Mary's information.

He was the same guide who had accompanied us two days ago and, seemingly based on that brief acquaintance, Vanessa had greeted him as a long lost friend with a beaming smile and a hug. However, he was an agreeable young man whose voice was a definite improvement on our other guide, being pleasant to listen to, even if his information was lacking in places, him being a mere novice compared to the lady we had endured yesterday.

We may have uttered a collective sigh of relief at seeing him and not "The Woman" as she had been referred to but it was generally thought that Vanessa's actions were somewhat over the top. There were a few muttered murmurs of 'hussy' as people noted her behaviour and Millie even tut-tutted but it gave me food for thought; was I being unfair on Enzo, if she did indeed greet all people, whether she did actually know them or not, with a friendly hug?

From the theatre we went to the old quarries, which had also at one time been used to house political prisoners. I flinched a little with this information as it reminded me of another possible felon whom I was trying hard (but unsuccessfully) to forget. There are several caves in the quarries, all now closed to visitors, except one large limestone cavern, named the Ear of Dionysius due to its shape, as it tapers at the top, and also because of its acoustics, such that whispers within its deepest depths can be heard clearly at the entrance. However, after regaling us with tales of prisoners held within it so that their murmured escape plans might be overheard, as well as the screams of tortured victims, our guide then proceeded to say that the shape of this cavern, once used for storage of water in Greek and Roman times, may not be a man-made feature after all but might in

145

fact be a natural canyon.

Later in the morning we proceeded into Syracuse itself for a brief tour, which included a visit to the cathedral on the island of Ortygia, the historical centre of the city which is situated at the island's tip and linked to the mainland by two bridges. The cathedral or Duomo is said to be the oldest Christian church in Europe. It started out life as a Greek temple being built around the skeleton of the Temple of Athena and several huge Doric columns ('Not more "Doris" columns!' I heard Millie mutter under her breath) can clearly be seen both inside as well as from the outside. It was also briefly converted into a mosque at one time before reverting back to a church in Norman times. I was gazing all around, noting the aforementioned columns -

I could not believe it. How arrogant can a man be? How conceited! After I had told him not to follow me again, there was Enzo lounging against a pillar inside the cathedral! Did he really believe that I did not mean it? Did he think that he could smile and use his Mediterranean charm and I would forgive him? True, Millie had suggested a plausible reason for him dropping the wine bottle but that did not excuse all his behaviour, and maybe Vanessa did just have an overly friendly nature.

As I stood there debating whether to go across and speak to him he turned his head and whispered something to a person standing next to him. From where I stood I could not see who his companion was and, curious, I carefully inched my way around a huddle of people until I had a better view.

Then wished I had not bothered. Vanessa was leant against him saying something and as I watched he placed one arm around her shoulders and then smoothed a lock of hair back from her face. She reached up and kissed him. Stunned I stood immobile while they chatted, for all the world like old lovers, smiling fondly at each other.

He had lied to me. He had known her before. I turned away and stumbled out of the dark interior of the church into the sunlight, any thoughts of forgiveness forgotten. The sudden brightness, like the realisation I had been a fool, overwhelmed me and I could feel my eyes begin to prickle with tears. No, I thought, for the second time in twenty-four hours, I will not cry; he's not worth it.

I allowed Millie to sweep me along for a quiet stroll through the town before we met back at the harbour in time to eat. Mary had again provided maps but I was not in the mood to decipher its hieroglyphic markings but as we only had a limited amount of time and nothing in particular that we wanted to see or do, we sauntered aimlessly about so as not to get lost and miss our meeting point. Thus, we would go up one side of the street gazing at the old buildings with their wrought-iron balconies and then walk back on the other side making sure we did not stray far from the harbour. From time to time Millie would point out an interesting building and I would obliging say, 'Oh, that's nice,' but my heart and my mind were elsewhere.

Lunch was booked on – or rather inside – a boat as we cruised the waters around the harbour. An appetising array of local foods was arranged across large wooden tables fixed to the floor of the vessel allowing us to walk around and help ourselves to whatever took our fancy. This we were able to wash down with wine, red or white, served by the crew who mingled amongst us carrying huge plastic containers from which they poured the contents into our outstretched plastic cups. It might appear to be slightly dubious unhygienic mass catering but I was in need of a drink, however small the plastic cups might be. However, the crew did later come amongst us offering refills; I think the size was more for ease whilst traversing the open water than for stingy rations; and despite all the plastic containers it tasted fine.

The trip along the sea wall and back again passed a couple of hours pleasantly enough. Somehow it had fallen out that Vanessa and I were sat along different areas of the boat so I did not have to sit and converse with her about various topics, which I would rather not mention and, of course, Enzo was not part of our group.

All the while from somewhere came piped music that sounded like possibly the Sicilian equivalent of our sea shanties and also some Italian songs that I recognised. As someone softly sang "*Sway*" the boat bobbed up and down and I hummed along, although

148

I tried not to listen too closely to some of the words. I did not want to sing romantic love songs; I would much prefer something along the lines of, "What shall we do with the drunken sailor?"

After all the amphitheatres and Greek temples Castello di Donnafugata made a nice change, although part of it was built in the fourteenth century most of it was constructed in the neo-classical revival style of the nineteenth century. Inside a myriad of tiny rooms were displayed articles of antique clothing many in glass cases, others behind a thick red cord roping off the area, in typical room set-ups complete with vintage furniture.

Millie and I were enthralled as we exited one room only to enter yet another equally lavishly laid out. In period settings against painted wall backdrops or authentic wallpaper stood well-dressed dummies in mostly nineteenth century costumes but I gazed in awe at an art deco style kimono-like dress from the early twentieth century. There were a couple of smartly dressed gentlemen in a billiard room and a lady ready to go horse riding, complete with side saddle. There were sumptuous gowns dripping with yards of lace, and beads, pearl necklaces, and such flamboyant feathers on hats! There were ladies sporting huge leg of mutton sleeves, and several severe looking ladies clothed head to toe in heavy black mourning outfits complete with thick veils.

Eventually and regretfully we came to the end, and

ventured outside. A wide stone staircase to one side of the building led up to a long walkway with views over the entrance area and the surrounding countryside where we stood for a while just gazing out over the landscape and discussing again the wonderful costumes we had seen.

Millie then decided she would prefer to potter a little around the grounds or sit awhile on a bench with Joan, and so I set out to explore further on my own. Which was undoubtedly a mistake.

I marched up the central path between the flower beds to a summerhouse at the end and then skirted around the edge and came to the maze tucked away in the corner. The maze is a little odd in that it is not the usual maze comprised of hedges but built entirely of solid grey stone. As I considered whether it was prudent to enter by myself Neil and Christine emerged from an opening.

'Don't be bashful,' Neil said in passing. 'You can do it.' He grinned and walked on.

I stood and contemplated the edifice before me. Mary had described it as "a small maze" and it did not look unmanageable for one person on her own. She had said we would know when we reached the centre, and then it would be easy to find our way out. Such a small maze could not be a problem, could it? I could manage to find my way to the centre and out again by myself, couldn't I?

I glanced at my watch. It was 3.30pm and we needed to be back at the bus, parked a little way down the road from the Castello at 4.15pm. If I left at

4pm it would give me time to nip in the ladies on the way to the bus; that left thirty minutes to traverse the maze; ample time, or so I thought.

I strode purposely forward. Should I have a system? I wondered, such as keeping to left hand paths or taking all the right-hand turnings? However, after several dead-end passages and retracing my steps I realised I was walking the equivalent of going around in circles. Patrick and Hilary, the couple whom I had sat next to on the plane and who I had seen chatting to the receptionist when we first arrived, appeared and then disappeared around a corner after a nod in greeting.

I came to another dead end, retraced my steps, back to another dead end, and that was when the panic started to set in. I looked at my watch 3.45pm. I had spent fifteen minutes walking from one dead end to another. I jumped up and down and looked after a section of wall that was lower than its neighbours. I spied Patrick's head retreating.

'Hello!' I cried, 'Can anybody hear me?'

There was no answer, despite the fact that I knew at least two other people were close by. They must have heard my cries for help. Why weren't they answering me?

Walking a little quicker I took another turning and came to another dead end. I retraced my steps and took another path, but soon realised I had tried this way, several times, already. I felt as if the walls were closing in on me.

'Hello! Is anyone there?' I called again. My heart

was thumping and tears were pricking behind my eyelids. I'm a grown woman, I thought, I'm not going to cry. Then the thought came unbidden, but you're lost, no-one knows you're here except two people who have ignored your cries and another couple who are by now probably far away. And you are running out of time.

I sniffed and started to run, getting desperate. Every now and then I would jump up and see if I could spy anyone else in the maze over the top of the wall. I continued to call out to no avail. I chided myself for foolishly thinking I could traverse it by myself; what an idiot.

By 4pm I was wiping away a couple of stray tears when I thought I heard footsteps coming from ahead. Someone was coming! I walked a little faster, sniffed again, trying to compose myself in front of a stranger, and walked smack into a man appearing quickly around a corner. I belatedly put my hands out to steady myself when two hands gripped the top of my arms firmly.

'Carrie! *Cara mia*, are you alright?'

I did not need to see his face to realise it was Enzo. I was so relieved I could have hugged him; in fact I did. I buried my face on his shoulder and wrapped my arms around him for a few seconds.

Slowly he unwound me and gently lifted my chin with his finger. 'Carrie?'

'I couldn't find the way out,' I mumbled, partly embarrassed, partly ashamed, very pleased to see him, but loath to admit it.

'It's here,' he said gently, turning and with an arm around my shoulder guided me the few remaining steps to the exit; I had been so close to finding my way out.

He accompanied me back to the main castle building talking all the time but in a way that helped further to calm me down. Once outside the maze he had removed his arm and we walked along without touching. Annoyingly, I found I could not shut him out of my life like turning off a tap; he continued to drip through into my thoughts. I realised that I really would not have minded if he had held me in his arms a little longer.

I asked him how he came to be in the maze, wondering if by chance he had been looking for me.

'I heard someone cry out for help,' he explained. 'I could not ignore a lady in distress. 'He smiled, white teeth flashing in his tanned face. I considered again how Patrick and Hillary could have ignored my plight – if Enzo heard me call out they also must have done, being already inside the maze and thus so much nearer.

Back at the castle we bumped into Millie outside the ladies' toilets and he handed me over to her care with a few explanatory words. Millie fussed over me like a mother hen all the way back to the bus. By 4.14pm I was safely in my seat, not late and not the last person to arrive, so my fears on that score were groundless. However, as I caught the eye of Patrick as he took his place and then quickly turned away looking a little guilty, I wondered again as to why they had seemed to have left me lost in the middle of the maze.

Millie asked me for the umpteenth time if I was alright and praised once more the actions of 'that handsome Sicilian,' and I found that my heart was still beating madly, even though I was no longer afraid.

For some of our group this was to be the final night of the holiday; for others such as myself we had signed up for an optional two night extension on Vulcano Island, one of the Aeolian Islands. I had been pleased to discover that Millie had also elected to stay on. I had my fingers crossed that Vanessa might be going home, a sentiment that I later had some cause to regret.

Chapter Ten

Thoroughly Modern Millie

After our arrival back at the hotel I felt the need for solitude and decided to take a walk along the coastal road to clear my head of conflicting thoughts. It had not taken long for Enzo to take up with Vanessa after our argument yesterday, and after their behaviour in the cathedral I was more than ever convinced that they had met previously and his protestations to the contrary were thus untrue.

But then he had come to my rescue in the maze. I had no idea where Vanessa had been at this time; obviously they had not been together. He had treated me with the utmost courtesy and I was truly grateful, without him I might still be stuck in the midst of the concrete maze now! My heart jumped again at the mere thought and I quickly increased my pace.

But I could not walk away from my feelings for Enzo. Despite his lies, his dalliance with another woman my heart still reacted to his smile, my body to his touch. Just for a moment I wished myself hundreds of miles away, back at home where he could not affect me with his presence.

On my way back to the hotel, despite my mixed feelings of anger and despair, I spied a small kiosk tucked away in the corner that I had passed without noticing earlier. As I still needed a replacement gift for Pat I took a couple of deep breaths to compose myself, counted to ten, and then entered its gloomy interior.

Once inside I decided that the darkness was for effect and not for any sinister reason of trying to disguise dodgy gifts or inflated prices or in any way confuse an unwary tourist. Recognising me as such, the little old lady seated on a stool in the corner ushered me further into the depths and gestured with wide arms for me to look around, and so I did, taking my time.

All the while the lady grinned encouragement but uttered not one single word, for which I was grateful; she seemed aware that tourists who are forever having items thrust inches from their noses for their inspection tend to only remain in such establishments a short time and quickly leave.

I had selected an engraved leather wrist band for my nephew, Greg, when I spotted the lava encrusted bottles tucked discretely to one side. This store owner obviously held the same opinion of these gifts as the average tourist, but displayed a small selection just in case anyone was rash enough to buy one.

Tentatively I poked through the assortment; one

bottle with an island and 'X' marks the spot of Etna, a grotesquely hideous Jupiter, king of the gods sporting an unruly full beard and hair that rivalled that of Medusa, Neptune holding his trident aloft in quite a threatening manner and a couple of erotically suggestive erupting volcanos, which had been tucked away at the back out of view. Just on a whim I checked but there was no Vulcan, blacksmith to the gods but there was, thankfully one bottle with Venus rising from her shell, almost identical to the bottle that Enzo had broken.

I inspected the bottle carefully just to check whether it looked like it had been in the back of the shop since Vesuvius had erupted over Pompeii and, as it looked clean and comparatively tasteful, I added it to my purchases along with a selection of postcards. The shopkeeper's grin widened as I laid the items on her tiny countertop, and offered '*francobolli*?' to which I nodded gratefully and confirmed '*Gran Bretagna.*'

Back outside the tiny shop I allowed myself a small smile and continued on my way back to the hotel.

After a dinner of dolphinfish, which had everyone once they had read the menu declaring they were not sure they wanted to eat it, until Paul confirmed that it was not actual dolphin, the friendly mammals of the sea, but a ray finned fish, which actually tasted like mackerel and was rather nice, accompanied with a mixed salad and pasta, Millie took me to one side and whispered that she thought we ought to have another look on the computer and gather our thoughts about Richard – and for a minute I thought she meant lanky Richard and that perhaps the close proximity to him on the back seat had pierced through her defences – until she had laughed and shook her head.

'No, not that Richard, King Richard,' she said, 'and Arthur; I just want to double check a few things. Besides,' she added with a gleam in her eye, 'I am happily married, have been for over fifty years,' which confirmed my estimation of her age. I again marvelled that she had thought about using modern technology when it might be suggested that someone of my more tender years might have done so; I put it down to my being distracted by other things. Or people.

However, Lanky Richard, as we took to calling him so as to distinguish him from other Richards of more royal blood, was in the computer room when we arrived, although I suspected that Mille had been aware of his intention to use the computer when she had suggested we do likewise. We hovered discretely in the doorway until he had finished and then at Millie's indication I slipped into the (warm) seat. Thankfully Richard had again left it set to English language for us.

'Are you alright dear?' Millie asked as I settled myself in front of the screen awaiting her instructions as to what to look up.

I nodded, not trusting myself to speak; it had been a day of mixed emotions. Millie took the hint and for once did not probe further, but merely produced a sheet of paper which was covered with tiny neat writing; her notes on the 'Richard situation,' which made me smile.

We consulted the paper on which she had laid out in chronological order the series of events that had taken place hundreds of years ago, starting with the Roman blacksmith Vulcano forging the swords in his workshop beneath Mount Etna. Unfortunately, we were in danger of being side tracked before we had barely started and with our time being limited, the computer being available to any other hotel resident who wished to use it, I had to chivvy Millie along.

However, we did discover an interesting fact about Vulcano or Hephaestus; it may have been unrelated to our Arthur/sword enquiries, but it was curious all the same. As Paul had previously mentioned, gods had tended to make people in their own image, and most people's views of the ancient gods are of beautiful, powerful people. Think of Venus, goddess of love, arising from her shell, and the contest held between the three goddesses for the golden apple, the prize for the one considered the fairest.

The blacksmith to the gods (who just happened to be married to Venus although she was unfaithful to him) was unique among them in that he was imperfect. He had crippled feet, which may have been due to an accident at birth or resulting from him being thrown from Mount Olympus by his mother Hera/Juno, wife of Zeus/Jupiter. The ancient Greeks, who revered him, kept dwarf-like statues near their hearths.

The mythic image of a lame smith is widespread and includes the Egyptian god of craftsmen, Ptah who is portrayed as a lame dwarf, as well as the lame Norse bronzeworker, Weyland the Smith. Bronze Age smiths added arsenic to copper to harden bronze especially if tin was scarce, thus many Bronze Age smiths would have suffered from arsenic poisoning and thus may have developed skin cancer as a result of their livelihood. The Bronze Age preceded the Iron Age and, as Hephaestus is an Iron Age smith, his disability may have been due to a lingering ancient folk memory.

I think Millie due to her skin condition felt some empathy with the disfigured god and I had to urge her to move on with the next item on her list; what became of the sword once it had been created. After Caliburn, the sword from the stone, broke Arthur replaced it with Excalibur from the lake. We decided not to get side tracked by mirages over the water and other paranormal, or normal, phenomena.

'So, what happened to the sword on Arthur's death?' Millie queried. 'That's what we need to check before we look at places where it may have turned up years later.'

Agreeing that this was a good idea, I entered the question and searching through the answers it appeared that Arthur had declared that the sword should be returned from whence it came. One of his knights from the Round Table carried out his dying wish, and after two abortive attempts, on the third try a hand appeared from the lake and drew the blade beneath its waters.

'Well, that's that,' Millie declared. 'The sword cannot he here in Sicily if it was thrown into the lake.'

'Ah, but was it?' I queried. 'Think about it – a valuable sword, which according to one source makes its owner the king of England, would you have thrown that away? Okay,' I said as Millie was about to object, 'its royal links might in a way make it too hot to handle, hence Arthur decreed that it should be returned to the lake and not passed on to his successor, which in a way is a little weird; I wonder who his successor as King of England was? Anyway, what if the knight made two or three half-hearted attempts to get rid of the sword but kept it? Or he might have waded into the water after Arthur's death and retrieved it? Let's not be too hasty to dismiss alternative scenarios.'

I turned once more to the computer screen and asked a few more questions. 'Ooh, what's this?' I brought up an intriguing newspaper article dated from a few years ago in which a child wading in Dozmary Pool in Bodmin, Cornwall, had found a sword. We eagerly read the piece until we came to the part where his father surmised it being probably a discarded film prop. We both slumped down in our seats as we considered the many Arthurian films that had been made in the vicinity over the years, meaning there were likely to be countless other swords just waiting to be discovered.

'Ancient people did throw items into lakes as offerings to their gods didn't they?' Mille said after

161

awhile. 'Celtic people, I think.' I nodded. 'Actually, thinking about it, the Hindus still do in India,' she added, 'and in some places such practises have resulted in quite a lot of pollution if the items thrown in are not natural; these days it is not iron swords that gets thrown in, but plastic! Ug!'

The location of Arthur's sword after his death being dealt with, we decided to move on to the next part of Millie's list. This jumped in time and brought us to Richard the Lionheart. It was probably undeniable that he stopped in Sicily on his way to the Holy Land during the crusades and that he stayed in Messina while attempting to sort out his sister's domestic situation. The question was – did he have the sword with him? As King of England, as noted, he might have had ownership of it. Would he have taken it with him on the Crusades?

'Would he have left it behind in England?' put in Millie. 'If it conferred kingship on its owner, would he have risked a rival trying to claim his throne in England?'

'Would he have taken it with the thought of using it as a gift in securing his sister's release? Or had he indeed handed over a duplicate, a fake?'

If the sword did indeed bestow kingship on its owner then we thought it unlikely that Richard would hand it over to a foreign king who might then be tempted to seize his crown as well. That left us with the possibility that the sword was a fake, which was a good reason to keep it hidden so that no-one could see that the Sicilian had been duped. In that case, why would anyone still be looking for it?

'To fool the Sicilian king it would still need to be a good quality sword,' Millie said. 'Maybe with a handle inlaid with jewels, that would make it valuable. '

I agreed with this reasoning. So where would it be hidden – a Norman castle in Sicily, not a church as we had agreed previously otherwise if a priest or someone holy found it they might claim it for the church, no it had to be a castle such as the one in Aci Castello or the Royal Palace in Palermo.

And there we floundered, but we did find one other interesting article concerning a mediaeval knight from Tuscany in central Italy who became a hermit. In 1180 a vision from the Archangel Michael instructed him to give up all material things, however the knight argued that would be as difficult as splitting a rock, and to prove it he stuck a nearby stone. The rock yielded, so it is said, like butter, and his sword was stuck almost up to its hilt. For centuries pilgrims and tourists (here we exchanged grins) flocked to the tiny chapel built around the sword where it could be seen with only its hilt, wooden grip and few inches of blade protruding. Thought by many to be a recent fake, the style and composition of the metal was recently dated to the twelfth century, as were two mummified hands kept inside the chapel. Legend has it that anyone who tries to pull the sword from the stone has their arms ripped from their sockets.

'Oh, that's charming!' commented Millie. 'I think I

prefer the English version.'

'It says here that his miracle indicated humility and holiness,' I pointed out, 'whereas Arthur's feat proclaimed his glory.'

'I'm still backing Britain,' Millie said. 'Anyway, what shall we look up next? I know, I would like to recheck the piece that mentioned Excalibur was recovered in the nineteenth century.'

I duly obliged, but for some reason, whatever word combinations I entered into the search field I could not conjure up the article we had read the other evening. I did, however locate further information regarding the suggestion, as mentioned earlier by Patrick, that the sword had been found by Richard's father, Henry II, buried with the bodies of Arthur and his wife, Guinevere, in Glastonbury in the late twelfth century. Glastonbury was thought by many people to be the location of Camelot, where Arthur held his court, although as it had at one time been a small island surrounded by water, it could also be the Isle of Avalon.

However, we discovered Henry's claim was viewed with suspicion for two reasons. Firstly, in the preceding years the usual influx of pilgrims to the abbey at Glastonbury had dwindled. The abbey had suffered a devastating fire a few years earlier and news of such a find would bring the pilgrims flocking back, bringing with them donations, and secondly, Henry was engaged in wars against the Welsh. People at that time believed that Arthur would one day return as king and rescue them in their hour of need, but if his body was found that would put an end to those beliefs. Nevertheless, in the early 1960s evidence was uncovered that a grave had been disturbed in the ancient church, although no-one knows who they were or what became of the bodies.

'So, do we assume that Henry really did find the sword, passed it to his son, who later gave it away in exchange for his sister?' Millie queried. 'That the last known location for the sword was indeed in Sicily?'

'That would imply that not only is the sword real but that Arthur and Guinevere, and all the Knights of the Round Table, were real people,' I replied. 'Not just stuff of myth and legends.'

'Well they found Troy, didn't they?'

I found I could not argue with that.

We decided next to move on to consider who might be searching for Arthur's sword – Dottie, Patrick and Hilary, Paul and Christine; Millie added Richard's name purely due to the fact that he had been following us around Aci Castello. And, of course, Enzo.

'Do you really suspect Richard?' I queried. 'I know he followed us around the castle but possibly that was because he thought we were acting suspiciously,'

Millie grinned, 'Which we were.'

'Which we were,' I agreed, also with a grin. 'But I don't think he was present when we had our evening chat in the bar about the sword. I know he is a bit of an oddball, always sitting in the middle of the back seat and making suggestive comments, but I think that's just it; he's odd.'

'But don't you ever wonder what he is doing all the time, forever on the computer of an evening? Do you really think he has that many family and friends whom he is emailing back home?' Mille asked. 'He must be using the computer to browse for some sort of information, only what?'

'I thought you hovered rather close, trying to look over his shoulder!' I was amazed at Millie's gall.

'Well, as Miss Marple always maintained, people overlook a little old lady, don't they?'

I gazed at Millie; I had always thought her to be just what she appeared to be – a little old lady.

'So, what are you really?' I asked. 'Retired from the secret service or whatever?'

This time Millie laughed out loud. Then she shook her head rather sadly. 'No just an old lady, a stay at home wife and mother, now grandmother. When I was your age women with families did not work, unless they were really desperate. We got married and we gave up our jobs to look after our children. Don't get me wrong; I love my children. But it was all rather boring at times.' The mischievous grin returned. 'This is such fun!'

We turned our attention to our other suspects. Dottie we decided was dotty; there was no other word for her. A little manic, possibly, but obviously a firm believer in all things Arthurian.

'But I think we do need to keep an eye on her,' Millie suggested, 'Purely because fanatics will go to any lengths to justify their, sometimes, crackpot beliefs. She may be searching for the sword, but a little harmless looking, as long as she does not ransack anywhere, is no problem. Her table manners, on the other hand…' Millie shuddered and left what she thought unsaid, nevertheless, I agreed with her.

Paul and Christine we soon dismissed as harmless. We had no idea of what Christine did for a living, possibly we surmised, she was a teacher like her husband. He had proved knowledgeable about the mirages over the water but that might just be an area of particular interest for him.

'What about Tom and Angela?' Millie asked. 'They were very keen to see the Royal Palace in Palermo.' I dutifully marked a query next to their names but could think of nothing significant to add other than he claimed to speak Italian.

Patrick and his wife I viewed with more suspicion. I agreed that our first meeting on the plane had not been auspicious but he had seemed rather too friendly with the receptionist for someone who had just arrived at the hotel that evening. I remembered how they had both instantly fell silent when I approached and turned to me as if I was an unwanted intruder on their conversation. Millie agreed.

'He does not strike me as a particularly friendly or chatty chap. His wife seems pleasant enough if rather insipid.'

'And,' I added with a shiver, 'they left me in the maze when I was lost. I cannot believe they did not hear me shouting for help. How can people ignore someone in distress like that?' For a moment I was transported back to the interior of the maze, the walls closing in on me.

That brought us to my other problem – Enzo, my saviour on this occasion.

'For once he was in the right place at the right time,' Millie said. I nodded not trusting myself to speak for a moment. 'After his earlier behaviour with Vanessa in the cathedral, yes I saw them as well, I must admit I am a little surprised that if he followed us to Donnafugata that he was not in her company again, draped over a bench or something insalubrious.' Millie paused and looked at me. 'No,' she said decisively, 'whatever made him associate with that hussy I cannot imagine, but I am sure, I really am, trust me as a mother of two now grown strapping sons and four grandsons with another on the way (and while I would like a girl this time, heaven help us if it is, as she would be a spoilt little miss and no mistake), I am sure Enzo is sweet on you. No, his dalliance with Vanessa is for some other reason. Oh!'

Millie clapped her hand to her mouth when she realised what she had said. If Enzo's and Vanessa's relationship was not on a personal level than it had to be on a professional one. And at that moment I could only think of one thing. Theft.

I had forgotten the newspaper clipping I wanted to translate. Millie had looked accusingly at me as if I had deliberately forgotten it as I did not want to discover that Enzo was a crook. Perhaps I was trying subconsciously put any such thoughts to the back of my mind, however if no-one hovered around us wanting to use the computer I suggested I could nip back to my room for it later; for the moment we decided to investigate the question whether there had been any recent burglaries. I duly entered the search details.

Then all other thoughts flew out of my head, as there on the screen in front of us was a tiny statue of Venus arising from her shell. There were similarities to the one portrayed on the bottle of wine I had purchased, not once but twice; they were not identical; the sweep of the arm was different, her hair tumbling over her shoulders was styled differently but even so, it was undeniably Venus, goddess of love.

Chapter Eleven

Volcano

I scanned the feature but could not make out any recognisable names. Then using the Italian into English translation facility on google I cut and pasted sections of the article and with Millie peering over my shoulder we read about the recent theft of a tiny ancient statue of Venus, the Roman goddess of love.

'Couldn't have been Enzo,' Millie was quick to defend him. 'Look, the theft was in Milan and Enzo has been in Sicily these past few days.'

Except, I pointed out, when we had been to Erice and Segusta and he claimed not to have been trailing us that day as these are hilltop places and his wounds were aching. I was unsure if the dates matched up; the newspaper article was a little vague as to when the theft had occurred. He could have easily flown to Milan and back in 24 hours I thought. My mind prompted me – hadn't Enzo mentioned a museum in Milan? Did that mean he was familiar with the city?

Because he had been there recently?

Millie considered this, then suggested, 'But with his wounds would he have been able to break in anywhere? I mean he could hardly walk.'

'Maybe his limp was exaggerated somewhat. For sympathy. An alibi?' I regretted once again that I had left the newspaper clipping safely locked away in my suitcase; I don't know why I did not keep it with me in my handbag but securely tucked away from prying eyes. Unfortunately, there was no way I could go and retrieve it now in order to translate it; our time was up on the computer and suddenly there was a queue of people outside waiting their turn before dinner.

I was pleased to discover that Millie had also signed up for the Aeolian Island tour extension, however not so ecstatic to find Vanessa also numbered within the party staying on for the extra days. In retrospect I should not have been surprised, as our base on the island of Vulcano was a luxury spa hotel and she announced that she aimed to spend the time lounging by the pool. In fact most of our group were transferring across to the island including Joan, Dottie, Tom and Angela, and Paul and Christine.

We waved goodbye to Mavis and Dilys, and a few other couples I had hardly spoken to all week, who were flying back to England. We also said goodbye to our coach and its driver at the port and proceeded to lug our cases and a miscellany of belongings onto the ferry, as we travelled across as foot passengers.

When the ferry arrived and the mass thronged on the quay surged forwards I just about managed to wheel my case up the gangplank but I failed miserably when it came to storing it in the shelving unit provided, being unable to lift it onto a shelf. However, there were more cases to store than available shelves and so many were parked as neatly as possible in the area. Once they had stored their luggage (which required an extra ticket) all passengers had to find a seat and remain seated for the duration of the trip. This was no pleasure boat trip with outside seating to view the journey's progress but a functional craft with only a few tiny windows offering little in the way of a view.

Our party was separated and spread throughout the main and lower decks where row upon row of hard plastic seats awaited us. Various members of the crew prowled around ensuring that everyone was seated and then we were off speeding towards the group of volcanic islands named after Aeolus, the 'Keeper of the Winds' who according to Homer's Odyssey gave hospitality to Odysseus and his crew for many months while they recovered from their time at sea during their ten year voyage home to Ithaca after the fall of Troy. Aeolus gave Odysseus a favourable wind, along with unfavourable winds secured within a bag. With such winds imprisoned, the ship should have enjoyed a calm, safe, direct passage home. However, his crew thinking the bag contained a fortune in gold and silver, opened it and the winds escaped, driving them back to the island.

As Mary had relayed this tale to us during the short journey to the harbour I considered whether this was an omen; I wondered if over the next few days we would encounter a calm safe passage through the remainder of our holiday, or whether any evil winds would prevail.

Once the ferry docked we then had to struggle in the melee to retrieve our cases and make our way down the gangplank and across to where a mini bus from the hotel awaited our arrival. We were informed of our room numbers and given the necessary WIFI code, if required, while a couple of burly helpers stowed our cases. At the hotel we were given a brief guided tour of the grounds and facilities, and then treated to a welcome drink with a selection of mini pastries, particularly cannoli, the tube shapes filled with creamy ricotta cheese.

I was allocated a room on the ground floor and was pleased to discover that Millie was next door to my left, however Vanessa was on my right. Unfortunately there also seemed to be some noisy boisterous children in the vicinity. When I say 'room' it was actually a suite with a lounge area between the bedroom and the patio. I pulled back the sliding doors and stepped outside. If I walked the length of the patio area and craned my neck I could just spy a sea glimpse complete with a view of Stromboli, another of the volcanic islands and one to which there was an excursion planned in the hope of seeing one of its reported nightly eruptions.

It was not the first time I had been allocated a suite whilst on holiday, even as a single traveller but I do still enjoy the luxury of a spacious set of rooms; I once stayed in a suite with two lounge areas which each had a television, as well as there being a set in the bedroom; unfortunately, none of them worked.

The rest of the day was free to fill with whatever we wished; as ever this put some people at a loss as they had no idea what it was that they wanted to do. Millie declared that she was not a really a lounge around the pool person and while I did not mind this form of relaxation for an hour two the time that stretched before us seemed too long; besides I had already read most of my book at the airport and not being much of a swimmer I looked for other activities.

'How about we take the minibus back into town and have a mooch around?' I suggested. 'Look at the shops, and have a bite to eat for lunch as I suspect the food here will be pricey.' This proposal was greeted with various nods of approval from Dottie and Joan. Millie said she had overheard some of the other couples intending to travel into town to eat as the food at the hotel was expensive.

'I would also like to see if I could walk up the volcano tomorrow morning, so if I could find the directions to it today, that would help time wise, as we also have the boat trip to Stromboli in the afternoon.' I added

'Why not do that walk now?' Dottie suggested. 'We've plenty of time, the rest of the day.'

I shook my head. 'It's much too hot now; better to

start early tomorrow morning before the full heat of the sun. I am not sure where the path is but it looked pretty exposed when we passed by earlier; there did not seem to be any trees or much shade.' There were murmurs of assent. 'The first minibus down in the morning leaves just before nine o'clock. We could catch that.'

The other ladies nodded agreement with this and there was a general consensus that it sounded nice and would I mind company? What could I say? I could hardly refuse and say I preferred to be on my own when at other times I had actively sought their company (well, Millie's)? Even though they were advancing in years these ladies had seemed very fit up to now, and while the proposed walk was up the side of an active volcano, it was according to my guidebook, a gentle climb, graded as "easy," as long as walkers wore sensible shoes.

It was only about a ten minute drive back into town. The driver pulled up at the harbour and everyone alighted. Stalls selling mainly cheap jewellery and other tourist tat lined the quayside. We strolled past but nothing caught my eye. A little further along we came to the hot spring mud baths, which appeared to be a writhing mass of squawking, squealing bodies and we stood and watched for a few minutes.

'Tempted?' Millie asked.

'I considered it,' I admitted, 'until Christine mentioned that the mud is sulphuric acid based and ruins your swimming costume, even if you try and rinse it through immediately afterwards. I think you're only supposed to stay in the pools for a short time so it's possibly too much effort.'

Dottie murmured agreement, while Joan nodded.

Millie admitted she was unsure whether to sample the water or not. 'My guidebook says it has therapeutic effects and leaves your skin feeling soft, although the smell may also be retained.' She gave a little grimace. 'It was one of the reasons I decided to come here, to try the waters and the mud. However, standing even this close, I am not so sure. And if it leaves people smelling of sulphur for the next few days, well! I might be left with no company for the rest of the holiday, with people going out of their way to avoid me!'

I had noted before Millie always wore long baggy sleeves, which covered her arms but sometimes fell back to reveal patches of rough dry skin, possibly eczema or psoriasis, I did not like to pry and ask her.

'Ah, yes, the smell,' Dottie said, as a gentle breeze blew and we decided it was time to move on, the smell becoming unpleasantly stronger for a few seconds.

'I stayed in a hotel on the banks of the Dead Sea for a few nights once,' I said as we strolled on. 'I immersed myself in the water a couple of times, but it was very stony on the bottom of the sea and, of course, it is impossible to swim, only float; but there was also a tiny indoor pool of the same Dead Sea water and I liked to use that. No-one else ever came in while I was there, so I had the whole pool to myself. I could just linger on the steps for a few minutes in the warmth and obtain the benefits of the water without subjecting myself to all the stones in the sea. It did leave my skin wonderfully smooth. The hotel was also a spa and offered expensive treatments but a group of us did try slapping on the mud from the water's edge,' I laughed at the memory. 'It had the same health benefits but without the damaging effects on our purses. And of course, neither the Dead Sea itself nor the mud smelt.'

Millie then thought that maybe she might ask at the hotel reception if they offered any spa treatments using the sulphuric acid mud, possibly in a slightly diluted form, and it might be something with which to fill the time before dinner.

'Of course, you might know if I have been successful or not by the pong,' she added.

There were a few gift shops in the town and also a post office and while Dottie queued for some stamps, 'I'm so sorry,' she had apologised, 'Always seem to leave it to the last minute,' Millie, Joan and I browsed for souvenirs. I bought myself a shot glass with a map of the Aeolian Islands printed on it.

Millie tried to make conversation with Joan to pass the time. 'What's Vanessa doing to keep herself occupied? Lazing by the pool?'

Joan nodded before confirming, 'She said she needed a rest after all the exertions this week.' Millie raised an eyebrow as I sniggered in spite of slight twinges of jealousy remembering her canoodling in the cathedral; Joan had been serious.

'Exertions!' Millie exclaimed. 'What exertions has that minx made this week? She passed on going up Mount Etna. Whenever I noticed her she was sitting down drinking coffee, or a glass of wine; hardly strenuous sightseeing!' Luckily Joan was saved from having to reply by Dottie's exit from the post office, murmuring, 'Sorry, long queue.'

We strolled one way up the main street then when the row of shops petered out turned and retraced our steps back the other way, passing the sulphur pool again, the smell heralding its presence before any sight (or sound of its occupants) came into view. Further along the road seemed to be the area of cafes and restaurants, reminding us that it was some time since breakfast, with only the light snack of cannoli with our welcome drink. We therefore moved on at a rather more sedate pace, stopping every few steps to examine menus, and peer at the people already seated to decide if a place looked popular enough that we might like to eat there.

Then we spied Paul and Christine in a pizza place and before we could say that they might not want any company Dottie had made a beeline for their table and was in some sort of conversation with the waiter regarding an adjoining table.

'We could quickly make a run for it,' Millie suggested, as Joan followed Dottie into the café. Despite her smile and the accompanying gleam in her eye I was not 100% sure she was joking.

Not being a huge pizza eater I opted for ricotta and spinach cannelloni but the others chose pizza with

Millie and Joan sharing one between them. With nothing to do for the rest of the day except laze by the pool we all elected to have dessert, rich Italian ice-cream of various flavours.

'Need to stock up some strength and muscle if I am going to be mountain climbing tomorrow,' Millie declared ordering rum and raison flavour with a grin.

Christine laughed. 'I think the mountainside will be a sea of British faces in various shades of red tomorrow if everyone who has professed a wish to actually decides to make the climb.'

After lunch following various road signs we proceeded to search for the beginning of the mountain path. Paul and Christine joined us professing a desire for a gentle walk after lunch. Even from a distance smoke could be seen rising from various sections. It was quite a trek, at first through the winding streets of the town, then along a straight main road into the countryside, before we reached our goal. I was glad that we had made the effort to find the direct route there so as to save time tomorrow.

After a cursory glance around there was nothing to do but retrace our steps and take the minibus back to the hotel. There I relaxed by the pool, feeling that I had earned a period of inactivity, and read the remainder of my book (I vowed that for my next holiday I would pack two books). Eventually I had a gentle swim in the pool, before dinner. Millie wandered off to reception to enquire about spa treatments and I did not see her again until later that evening.

I allowed my eyes to close in the heat of the day. I had not seen Vanessa all day (good riddance, I thought) but neither had I seen Enzo; did I miss him? Or was I glad to have left him behind on the mainland?

The bathroom in my suite was very modern, top of the range, complete with a choice of a fixed shower head or a removeable one, but, for some strange reason, no door enclosing the cubical, so when I washed before dinner I flooded the room and had to mop the spillage up as best I could using the bath mat and some spare towels.

I had met Millie in the bar for a pre-dinner drink where announced she had enjoyed her spa treatment and thanked me for the suggestion.

'I feel quite rejuvenated, years younger. My skin positively tingles,' she said with a grin, looking around at the staff. 'All I need now is a young Sicilian toyboy!'

After a dinner of spaghetti with squid in black ink sauce, which tasted nicer than it sounded, and a stroll around the extensive grounds in the warm moonlight with my dinner companions, I was looking forward to relaxing in my room, perhaps to read a chapter of a book I had found in a small alcove library in the bar before I retired for the night.

I was further pleased to find on returning to my room that the noisy children in the area were asleep and all was quiet and peaceful, as one would expect when staying in an exclusive resort.

The noises started about 11.30pm just as I was just drifting off to sleep. I thought it rather late for someone to be taking a shower or washing their hair but assumed the disruption to my peace and quiet would be short lived. However, the repeated short bursts of water continued for almost an hour and a half, at roughly ten or twenty minute intervals. It sounded like someone taking a power shower as opposed to a toilet flushing as it did not seem to be followed by any sounds of a cistern refilling. Eventually in the early hours I drifted off to sleep only to be awakened again shortly after five o'clock by the constant bursts of water that seemed to emanate from above.

I got out of bed, slipped on my sandals and wondered over to the bathroom area where I stood and waited for the noise to recur again. After a few minutes there it was again; a blast of water from above, echoing down through a grill in the hallway. I paced around listening; after about fifteen minutes the noise came again: a few seconds blast of water.

I went back to the bedroom area and phoned reception however, the man on the other of the line, whilst being very polite, did not really understand my plight. Was there someone in the room above me? I wanted to know, or was it empty? I was concerned that there might be some sort of leak or fault; but the man could not tell me. Hanging up the phone, I sighed and decided to pack my bags. We might be staying in this hotel for only two nights but I was definitely only staying in this room for one!

By six o'clock I was packed and ready to swap rooms. I was in the process of checking around to make sure that in my weary state I had not missed anything, (not that I had unpacked everything for only a two nights' stay in the first place) when I was distracted, this time, by a noise coming from outside.

I had left the sliding doors open the merest fraction for some fresh air despite the room being on the ground floor as the patio area was surrounded by a low wall about waist height. Thinking perhaps a local cat might be on the prowl I went to investigate; I certainly did not want any stray wild life coming into the room to add to my woes.

There was certainly a Tom cat on the prowl but this one was just leaving, not entering. I don't know why I was surprised to see the man climbing over the wall marking the end of Vanessa's patio. The early morning sun glinted off his grey locks. He must have had quite a night (not that I had heard anything but then I had been distracted by constant running water) as he was making quite a mess of clambering over such a low wall; I would have expected a renowned cat burglar to be more than capable of scaling much taller obstacles with ease, even with a bad leg.

I gritted my teeth, refusing to utter the oath that I was thinking, and returned to checking I had packed everything. No, I did not want to stay another night in this room, next to Vanessa.

*

182

I stopped by reception on my way to breakfast and spoke with a very obliging young man who expressed concern that there were problems with my room and assured me there would be no difficulty in swapping to another. When I further informed him that I would be out all day, and unsure of when I would return, but not likely until sometime this evening, the smile slipped a little. However, when I added that my case was already packed he happily assured me that they would move it to my new room for me and I should just ask for the key on my arrival. I thanked him, handed over the existing key and proceeded on my way to breakfast.

I selected a table with a panoramic view of the grounds, overlooking the sea and with glimpses of the nearby island of Lipari. I contemplated the planned activities for the day; after eating an early breakfast I would doubtless be hungry again after a strenuous mountain climb but also needed an early lunch because we were due to meet at 2.30pm for the boat trip around the nearby islands on our way to Stromboli for a quick visit, a bite to eat there and then a leisurely return in the evening when the highlight would hopefully be a mini eruption of the active volcano.

I had eaten muesli with locally made yoghurt and was just finishing my bacon, eggs and mushrooms when Millie appeared. I assured her I did not mind if she sat with me; I was not leaving yet awhile as I was considering the pastries and fresh fruit, and a second cup of tea.

'Most important to keep hydrated in this heat,' she agreed. 'A second cup of tea is imperative,' and she left to peruse the fare on offer. She returned with some juice, cornflakes and Joan.

The ladies were very bright and chatty, well Millie was, not so much Joan, considering it was early in the morning and I decided that they had probably had more sleep than I had.

'I think Enzo reminds me of Cary Grant,' Millie said. My mouth full with a maple syrup pastry I looked at her for clarification. 'He was in that film, you know, ah, "*To Catch a Thief.*" Oh!' I stared hard at her and she became a little flustered realising what she had said. 'And others. He was in lots of others. Let me see, ah…' But here her memory failed her.

'"*Vertigo*,"' suggested Joan only to correct herself, 'No, that was James Stewart. "*Arsenic and Old Lace.*"'

'Oh, yes that's right, the one with the aunts,' Millie agreed, 'and lots of others. Comedies, I think, romantic comedies…' she looked around for inspiration.

At this time in the morning there were more members of staff in the breakfast room than there were guests; presumably the rest of our group were enjoying a lay-in, and just as I thought this Dottie appeared in the doorway, spotted us and ambled over.

'Morning ladies, mind if I join you?' We nodded and murmured agreement. The table was set for four places so there was no difficulty, other than for some reason she needed to pick up and move various cups and items of cutlery as well as the salt and pepper until she had it to her satisfaction. I was glad I had just about finished eating.

'Still intent on mountain climbing today, Carrie?' Millie asked, rescuing her cup and refilling it from the tiny pot.

'After all that inactivity yesterday I think I need the workout. We have done a lot of sitting on the bus and eating pasta this week so a little strenuous exercise would not go amiss.' Millie agreed that a 'little exercise' was ideal.

The other ladies concurred with this and there was a general consensus that as previously suggested, attempting the climb in the early morning before the heat of the day became intense was best.

Thus, it was agreed that we would meet in the grounds to take the first minibus supplied by the hotel to transport its guests into the local town at eight thirty. I decided I would leave the ladies to finish their breakfast as if I tarried any longer I might be tempted to drink a third cup of tea and went to explore the grounds and take a few photographs.

The hotel complex was situated on the coast with many little meandering paths leading down to natural swimming pools each with ladder access directly into the sea. For those less adventurous there were two outdoor pools surrounded by loungers with sumptuously thick padded cushions shaded by coordinated umbrellas. There were palm trees, giant cactus and other exotic plants I had no idea what they were. Even at this early hour a couple of women were lazing by one of the pools being served drinks by a handsome young man in a pristine uniform.

I glanced at my watch and noted I just had time to return to reception and use the ladies before the proposed trip into town; as I had handed over the key I could not return to my room to freshen up. When I arrived at the bus departure area Millie was already there with Joan standing silently by her side. There were two other couples also waiting. The driver arrived and allowed us to take our seats. Dottie came bustling up, a little breathless just as the driver was revving his engine.

'I'm sorry I'm late,' she wheezed. 'I could not find my sun hat. I thought if we are mountain climbing and it is exposed, I shall need a hat.'

We assured her that she was not late and indeed the driver waited another three minutes, and after Paul and Christine hurried over professing they thought that they might have been too late and missed it, he closed the door and set off.

It was only about a ten minute drive into town. The driver pulled up at the harbour and everyone alighted. Paul and Christine immediately strode off purposely towards the town. With the three comparatively elderly ladies I walked at a rather more sedate pace, again passing the tourist stalls but this time hardly sparing them a second glance. There were a few people in the hot spring mud baths and, again we stood and watched for a few minutes. As it was early, barely nine o'clock, the area was not as packed with people as on the previous occasions when we had passed by later in the day.

By tacit agreement we then turned our attention to the volcano. Having sussed out the direct route yesterday we were able to immediately stride out purposely in the right direction, without the usual dithering to discover whereabouts the mountain path began. Once we reached our destination we took a few photos and admired the large local cactus plants in the vicinity, I think more to allow Millie, the eldest in our group, a little time to compose herself. Then we commenced the climb.

To begin with the path was fairly broad and easy going although it was comprised of black volcanic gravel that caused us to slip and slither if we were not careful. Mary would have been very pleased with us as we all wore sensible solid shoes but even so we still trod with care.

'The chimney of Vulcan's workshop,' exclaimed Dottie after a while, seeming to live up to her name. 'That's what the Roman's called this whole island.' She suddenly stopped and twirled around causing little rivulets of pebbles to cascade down the slope. 'Hence its name "Vulcano" after Vulcan, the Roman god of fire.'

'Save your breath for the climb,' I heard Millie mutter.

'Furthermore,' Dottie added unperturbed, 'they believed that the island expanded due to volcanic eruptions as the foundry was cleared of ash and cinders as he worked.'

Gradually the ascent grew steeper, the turns

became less sweeping and the track became narrower. We stopped at various bends in the path to admire the view and catch our breath. Even though it was mid-morning the sun beat down from a cloudless blue sky and, as Dottie had previously pointed out, we were exposed to its full force being out in the open. Occasionally there was a slight cooling breeze but I was glad to have brought a water bottle.

The view was magnificent, stretching out over the island and also far out to sea; I could see some of the other islands including Stomboli, our afternoon destination. The sea and the sky were clear blue; the houses of the town, tiny dots. It was all very pleasant and peaceful. Occasionally other walkers passed us by, either descending having already reached the top and walked around the crater, or were younger, fitter or just in a more of a hurry and overtook us, nevertheless they all greeted us with a cheery 'Good morning' in a variety of languages.

When we reached approximately half way there was a signpost marking the spot with a little wooden bench. We all agreed it was time for a well-earned rest and with a few accompanying groans, our weary bodies obviously being unused to such strenuous exercise, we sat and greedily reached into our bags for refreshment.

I did not want to sit for too long in case my aching joints seized up; I wanted to continue the walk for as far as possible; I doubted we had time to reach the top and walk around the crater. We were only half way and, although the descent would obviously be easier, we did not want to rush unnecessarily and slip on the loose shingle; we also needed to leave time for the not inconsiderable walk back into the town centre for lunch before we embarked on our afternoon boat trip.

Millie was obviously having similar thoughts as she turned to me and said, 'I am not sure I shall go much further; I doubt the view will be very different from this, the same only from a higher perspective. Besides, I think the path is becoming narrower with larger boulders to navigate and I don't think I can do it.'

In the end the decision to continue or not was decided for us; I rose from the bench and started along the path to determine if I could judge the steepness and difficulty of the way just around the next bend. Millie was standing a little behind me. Joan had walked back a few steps to where two large boulders had almost blocked the path and we had had to squeeze between them to in order to proceed. She was, I think, leaning on one to enjoy the view when I heard her cry out whilst at the same time there came the sounds of slipping and sliding, the slither of gravel as she fell.

Luckily, she did not fall far. Some sections of the path bordered a sheer drop down the volcano side, at other points were little gullies, some deeper than others, and I shuddered to think what would have happened if she had fallen into one of these areas. As it was, she lay sprawled across the path with her leg protruding through the gap between the rocks, her right foot at a slightly odd angle. Dottie stood slightly to one side looking helpless.

Millie and I rushed across, but careful all the same on the uneven ground.

'Can you move?' Millie asked. 'Sit up?'

'Don't try to stand immediately,' I advised. 'Give yourself a chance to relax and recover from the shock.'

'My ankle,' was all that Joan could say, although admittedly she never said very much anyway.

Millie rushed straight into action and I had to put a warning arm out to prevent her from slipping as well. From her backpack she produced a linen scarf that she proceeded to douse in water from her drinking bottle before laying it across the stricken woman's brow. After a few minutes when Joan was able to sit upright without any dizziness or other side effects Millie redampened the cloth and this time wrapped it around Joan's injured ankle, which had already started to swell. We debated whether we should try and remove her shoe, but without it how could she hobble back down the slope? There was no way that the three of us remaining upright could carry her. Unfortunately, or fortunately as Joan was temporarily blocking the path, there were no other people in sight to whom we could apply for aid, which was typical as there had been numerous people walking by earlier.

After a few more minutes we helped Joan into a standing position and then eased her over to the wooden bench, where she sat forlornly but out of the way of anyone who might possibly pass by. We waited patiently until Joan declared that she felt better and her ankle only throbbed a little bit, and indeed after the application of the cold compress the swelling had abated, however even in the full heat of the sun she looked pale. Possibly the injury had looked worse than it actually was when I had first seen her lying sprawled across the path but I still insisted she swallow a little more water before we attempted the descent; I did not want her collapsing of heatstroke as well.

We debated whether I should try and go on ahead in order to summon some assistance from somewhere in town but Joan assured us she could manage a slow walk back down the path. Her ankle was fine, she claimed, it had just been a bit of a shock, that was all. Although she looked askance at Dottie when I suggested she put her arms around mine and that lady's shoulder's for support, as Millie was the oldest and most frail in our group – other than Joan herself; Dottie's physique was built like an ox - Joan did as she was bid and we inched our way slowly downward.

After about twenty minutes of this snail like progression with Joan trying but failing to suppress little whimpers of discomfort we heard the approach of people from behind us. We moved carefully to the inner edge of the path to give them room to pass by, however it turned out to be Paul and Christine who immediately stopped and offered assistance. It was then that the unwanted thought crept into my brain –

where are you Enzo, when we need you?

Paul replaced me as support for Joan and we proceeded a little quicker along the route until we reached nearly to the bottom and there was only a gentle gradient when he decided it might be easier if he carried her until we reached the main road. We were lucky in that we were debating the best way get Joan back to the hotel when Christine spotted a vacant taxi cruising along and using very basic Italian managed to arrange for Joan and Millie to be transported back to the quay where they could take the next minibus back to the hotel.

The rest of us walked back and once we reached the outskirts of the shopping area Paul and Christine bid us farewell and that left me with the prospect of having lunch with Dottie, something that I was not particularly keen on.

It was not just her personal habits and her apparent lack of hygiene or awareness of personal space that concerned me, but on the walk back into town after Joan had been ensconced inside the taxi with Millie and had appeared to settle back and relax, it occurred to me that up on the hillside she had been more than a little wary of Dottie; she had even seemed almost afraid and had shrank from that woman's touch when she had aided her down the slope. Okay, so Joan's apparent relaxation in the taxi might have partly been due to being nearer to the hotel and off the hillside but it also seemed to correlate with having Millie beside her and not Dottie.

Besides, if Dottie started lecturing again on Roman gods and volcanos I was not sure I could bite my tongue; normally such topics would interest me, but at the moment I had other things on my mind. Like food.

We needed to find somewhere for a quick lunch before our boat trip. As we strolled along a street lined with eateries I wished Paul and Christine were still with us, and not just for their company, as Christine's Italian would come in handy. Finally, we spotted a restaurant situated a little further back from the street that seemed secluded and shady, with the added bonus that the menu was laid out in four languages, including English. A quick perusal revealed it to be reasonably priced and both Dottie and I declared we had spotted dishes that appealed and so we entered.

A portly gentleman (was that a good sign? I wondered) ushered us over to a small table and produced menus which he left us to consider for a few minutes. I ordered ravioli containing grouper with melon and almonds, and Dottie decided to have tagliatelle with salmon in a cream sauce. After our strenuous walk in the hot sun we added a large bottle of sparkling spring water, and then I also decided to have a lemon sorbet. The food was delicious and for once Dottie seemed less inclined to handle everything in sight. Perhaps Joan's accident and the fact that it could have been more serious had finally hit her and she sat and ate quietly, intent on her food.

'Did Cary Grant have curly hair?'

193

Dottie stopped eating and stared at me, her fork hovering in mid-air.

'I'm sorry,' I apologised. 'It was just something that Millie said earlier and I just wondered…' I tailed off lamely.

However, Dottie replied as if I had asked a sensible question. 'No, I don't think so; unless he was wearing a wig of course.'

'Yes, that must have bit it,' I said, not at all sure.

We had been informed the boat would leave at 2.30pm and so just after two o'clock I gestured to the waiter for the bill, which he brought some quarter of an hour later, just as I was beginning to panic, it being a good ten minutes' walk to the quay. We had taken it in turns to visit the ladies, movement which I think suggested to him our imminent departure. We had our money ready and thrust the notes in his direction as we headed towards the exit.

Millie waved to us from the boat as we walked by unsure as to which was our particular vessel. We hastily clambered aboard gratified to be informed that we were not last. While Dottie remained on the main deck with Tom and Angela I climbed up to the top deck where Millie had saved me a seat.

'How's Joan?' I asked as I settled myself, pleased that Dottie had found new companions.

'Resting by the pool with Vanessa,' Millie replied. 'She had not signed up for the trip anyway; apparently small boats make her a little queasy.'

I nodded. Even in the gentle swell while docked at the quay we were bobbing up and down. Mary appeared counting heads and seemed satisfied. It was not a private boat trip and there were a handful of other tourists aboard. We set sale, first to Lipari to pick up more passengers, on our way to Stromboli, the volcanic island where Jules Verne had ended his story "Journey to the Centre of the Earth" with his intrepid explorers propelled back to the surface through the active volcano.

There was quite a stiff breeze in the open water that made conversation a little difficult at times especially when we hit a larger wave, even so Millie expressed that she was glad not to have Dottie's company and her incessant conversation about Romans and volcanos.

'Gosh, does that make me sound mean?' she asked. I shook my head as we giggled.

Stomboli, Mary had told us, is nicknamed "the Lighthouse of the Mediterranean" due to the frequent eruptions of its volcano – hence our trip – that can be seen from many locations around the island, much like its counterpart, Etna on the mainland.

When we eventually arrived Mary led us up a narrow twisting road to the house, marked by a plaque, where the actress Ingrid Bergman lived with Roberto Rossellini while making the film "Stomboli" in 1950. Their affair had caused quite a scandal at the time, she said.

We had a little free time to wander around and then Millie and I met up with Paul and Christine and we went for an early dinner in a pizza restaurant before making our way back to the boat. Again, Millie insisted on sitting on the upper deck and I was glad as although it became decidedly cooler as the sun slipped low in the sky we were treated to the spectacle of a lone yacht silhouetted against a magnificent yellow sunset.

We sailed around the island and then, in an increasing gathering of boats of all shapes and sizes the captain cut the engine, and we waited. Little puffs of smoke or steam occasionally rose in the night sky from a crater visible near the top of the volcano, with smaller wisps emitted from the surrounding area. We lingered patiently at first, and then a little more restlessly as the mountain refused to provide us with any more exciting fireworks.

Eventually the captain started up his boat once more; it was time to return to Vulcano, dropping off those that had boarded at Lipari on the way. Of course, as we pulled away the volcano erupted in a little burst of fire. A cheer went up and everyone turned to view the diminishing spectacle behind us, the bright sparks illuminating the night sky, as we sailed away.

I joined in the gaiety, applauding the show like everyone else, then as I turned back to look in the direction in which we were traveling the darkness before us seemed suddenly ominous, as if we were leaving the joys of a holiday behind and a grim time lay ahead.

Back on Vulcano the hotel minibus was once more on

the quay ready to transport us to the hotel. I agreed to meet Millie in the bar for a quick nightcap but first I needed to settle into my new room. I was pleased when I enquired at reception to be told my replacement room was ready, my case had been moved, and I was handed the key.

I briefly surveyed the room. It was smaller than the previous one having no lounge area and no view, overlooking woodland at the back of the hotel, but the shower was a proper cubical with a door – and all seemed quiet.

I headed back to the bar passing Vanessa on the way.

'Not staying for a drink?' I asked politely, in an effort to remain friendly.

She shook her head, then grinned. 'I'm meeting someone later,' she said, raised her eyebrows and made a little face like it was a huge secret and wild horses wouldn't drag a name from her, in much the same manner as she had previously nipped inside the shops in Taormina but refused to divulge for what. 'You'll never guess!' she cried with glee, and with a sinking feeling I thought, I bet I can, recalling the glimpse of the grey haired man I had seen clambering over the patio wall this morning.

Little did I know that I would be the last person to speak to Vanessa that evening. Excepting, of course, that one person.

Chapter Twelve

The God of Fire

I slept well with no noises of running water, no crying babies and no sounds from either of the neighbouring rooms. I managed a shower without flooding the nearby area, and succeeded in avoiding Dottie at breakfast. Things were looking up, I decided.

Joan was also looking better and hobbling about with the aid of a stick that one of the receptionists had produced from unclaimed lost property. However, she frowned when Vanessa's name was mentioned as we waited in the lobby for the minibus to take us and our bags to the harbour to catch the ferry back to mainland Sicily.

No-one it appeared had seen Vanessa that morning.

After phoning her room and getting no reply Mary persuaded the hotel duty manager that she needed to check that Vanessa was not lying ill in her room, too sick to phone for assistance. However, when the door was opened it was apparent that Vanessa was not there, her bags lay unpacked with clothes strewn about the room, and her bed had not been slept in.

Any mumblings of concern for her welfare were replaced by muttering of discontent at her selfishness at keeping us waiting when we were due to depart; it was fortunate that there was more than one ferry each day to the mainland. I was reminded of the first day when she had kept disappearing into shops, keeping me and Joan waiting. How long ago that seemed now.

Various members of staff set off to search the hotel grounds while our group racked their brains as to when we had last seen her. I remember her comment about meeting someone late last night.

'I don't know who,' I told Mary, feeling myself blush a little as I could give an educated guess, as could probably anyone in our party, 'and I don't know where she was meeting him-' although she had not specified, I was sure it was a man '-and I don't know when, other than it was late last night.'

Of course, no-one in the group admitted to having a late night rendezvous with Vanessa. Questions were also asked of the staff, particularly the young bar staff, but all shook their heads.

It was almost an hour later when one of the groundsmen appeared, looking a little pale despite his natural tan, and spoke urgently to the duty manager who then approached Mary, a worried expression replacing his normal affable look. Vanessa had been found, he thought. Or rather a woman's body had been spotted in the sea, in one of the natural bathing areas; one arm had caught, hooked over the steps leading down into the ocean, hence it had not drifted away.

The rest of the morning became a blur. We were ushered as a group into a vacant conference room, our luggage was locked in a storage area, whilst we awaited the police. Further details emerged. Vanessa had been fully clothed in the water; she had not gone for an early morning swim (a late night swim in the dark was discounted as even Vanessa was not that idiotic). The cause of death was not divulged but rumours suggested it was not natural; no-one actually uttered the word "murder" but it was on everyone's mind.

When it was my turn to be questioned I could add nothing to the information I had given earlier to Mary. Vanessa said she was meeting someone, that was all I could swear to.

As I left the interrogation room, feeling a little nauseous and my hands somewhat sweaty, I wondered if the policeman suspected I was with-holding information; I assumed Vanessa had met the same person whom she had entertained in her room the previous night. However, I had the strange feeling that voicing my suspicions aloud might make them fact. It was one thing to suspect Enzo of burglary but another to suppose he might be guilty of murder.

I shuddered when I considered the same hands that had held me and comforted me after I had been lost in the maze might also have taken the life of another young woman. I would not want him to touch me again.

After we had all provided statements we were allowed to leave the conference room to saunter about the hotel grounds, excepting the bathing area down to the ocean, which was roped off.

Millie suddenly turned to me and said, 'You know, I have not seen Enzo for a couple of days. Not since we have been on the island.' I stared at her. 'I don't think he has been here, you know.'

'There are other hotels; ours is not the only one,' I pointed out. I hesitated, then told her about Vanessa's night-time visitor.

'And Enzo is not the only man with grey hair,' Millie said nodding towards where Tom and Paul stood chatting with Patrick, the man I had sat next to on the plane.

I opened my mouth to say something, but nothing came out. I stared at the group of three men, at Millie, and then my eyes roamed over the rest of our group, of which about 75% had greying hair; there were a couple of bald heads, a dark one, a blond, two completely white and one ginger.

Had I assumed that Enzo had been Vanessa's nocturnal visitor because I had expected it to be him? Enzo was young and fit, despite his grey hair – would he not have made a better job of clambering over the patio wall, even after his fall from his bike? I took a few steps nearer to the group of men to see them clearer, but it was no good, in the early morning half light I thought I had seen Enzo but none of the men from what I could see now jogged my memory.

'I saw them kissing in the church,' I reminded Millie, 'in a *church*!'

'And I am sure,' she replied, 'that if that was so, he had a good reason.'

I did not want to speak ill of the dead. I cast my mind back to consider whether Vanessa had kissed Enzo or whether Enzo had in fact kissed her, but my memory would not focus on the incident; there had been the pillar obscuring my view and I had left immediately I had noticed them.

Millie suggested we walk on some more, exercise being good for the brain.

'You sound like Miss Marple,' I told her smiling. Then remembered Vanessa and composed my face into a more appropriate expression. I may not have particularly liked her but she deserved a little consideration.

'When you get to my age it is considered by some to be an achievement and you get accorded some respect.'

I could not tell if she was joking. 'Many cultures revere their elders, that's true,' I said, 'more so than the British I fear.'

'Hence all the traditions of ancestor worship,' she added. We walked on a little in silence. The sun beat down from a blue sky, a few hotel guests lazed by the pool, life continued much the same. 'The thing about Miss Marple, as I mentioned to you before, is that people tend to overlook a little old lady.' She stopped and looked at me askance.

'So, what are you then? A master criminal in disguise?' I grinned. 'The retired head of MI5 or whatever?'

Millie laughed. 'No, nothing like that. But Enzo trusted me, I think,' she said but had the grace to look a little confused. 'He gave me something to look after. Would you like to see it?'

I opened my mouth to say 'Yes' but nothing came out. Enzo trusted Millie with something? She had said it casually but by interference the "thing" sounded important or valuable, or both. I was a little hurt that he had chosen Millie and not me, but then I had told him not to bother me, and I was not a harmless looking little old lady that some might overlook. Then I remembered the newspaper clipping and Tom's comment that Enzo was a burglar, a thief.

'Are you sure this "thing" is his? He hasn't stolen it?' I asked concerned, after all Mille was a little old lady, maybe she was a little too trusting of people. I remembered her comments about Cary Grant and the film he had made, *To Catch a Thief.* Just who was the thief, I wondered, Enzo or some unknown person, and who was doing the catching.

'Perfectly,' she declared. 'He showed me his – ah hem – credentials,' she joked, 'and swore me to secrecy.'

'Then perhaps you should not show,' I suggested, intrigued all the same, but she had already stopped and was rummaging in the rucksack that she always carried. She lifted the item carefully out of her bag, just as I became aware of footsteps behind me. The object looked like the bottle of skin lotion she often carried and I was unsure what was so special about it that she had wanted to show it to me now.

Before I could shout a warning that we were not alone someone rushed past, pushing me out of the way and snatched both Millie and the scarf wrapped around the article that she held carefully with both hands.

I stared at Tom, noting how the sun glinted off his grey hair reminiscent of Vanessa's nocturnal visitor, hair that was merely wavy as opposed to Enzo's curls.

With one arm around Millie's chest securing her arm clutching the scarf, he said, 'Mine, I think,' and with his free hand he started to roughly uncurl her fingers.

'Oh Millie!'

I had not heard him approach but I recognised his voice; Enzo was on the island after all.

Then I heard more approaching footsteps, heavy loud steps that heralded the approach of Dottie. Millie started to struggle in Tom's grasp and both she and her captor fumbled at the scarf and whatever it held.

'The sword!' cried Dottie.

'What sword?' I asked, turning to her in a mixture of disgust at her lack of concern over Millie's blight, and incredulity over what she thought the other woman clutched hold of, just as the bottle slipped from its covering and fell to the ground.

I expected it to shatter on impact, as had the bottle of wine I had bought, however it broke more or less in half, with a few tiny loose shards and a scattering of rock fragments and just a dribble of red wine. After roughly thrusting Millie aside Tom bent and retrieved something from the pieces; I had the merest glimpse of white before he quickly secreted it in his jacket pocket.

I stood frozen to the spot as Enzo rushed to Millie's side and helped her stagger a few steps across the grass a safer distance away from Tom. The woman seemed distraught, apologising to him for what had transpired.

Tom reached into his pocket and extracted a packet of cigarettes, calmly selected one and then produced a lighter. He took a couple of steps backwards and I noted behind him, tied to the ladder in one of the natural bathing areas was moored a small boat.

Safe in Enzo's clasp Millie turned around just in time to see Tom flick the lighter and a lick of flame appeared instantaneously.

'Oh, no!' Millie cried pointing. 'My scarf!'

We all looked at the scarf that had once held the bottle, now wound around Tom's left arm, not realising her concern. Tom took another step back, almost at the ladder, raised his arms, one holding the cigarette, the other the lighter and proceeded to calmly light his cigarette as if taunting Enzo to try something.

Then my vision of Tom was obscured by a

writhing wall of red as the scarf instantly caught alight and huge flames rose skywards. I instinctively took a step back and turned away, as much from trying to avoid the heat as the horrendous sight. I heard Millie whimper. Then all I could hear was the roar of the flames, the crackle of burning. And Tom's cries.

One of the Italian policemen, who had been patrolling the grounds searching for evidence of Vanessa's final hours, appeared and threw a wet towel over Tom before launching himself at the stricken man's legs. A second policeman appeared with more wet towels appropriated from beside the pool, while another advised Millie, Dottie and myself to leave the area. I needed no further urging.

Millie was inconsolable at the thought that she – or rather her scarf – had inadvertently been the cause of a man's death. Despite the swift action of the Italian police Tom had sustained severe facial burns, however Enzo informed us, it was likely that he had died of heart failure from the shock. A post-mortem would confirm this.

But the elderly woman remained distraught. 'I'm sorry Enzo,' she said in a small voice, 'I should not have removed the bottle from my bag; after all you entrusted it to me for safekeeping. I just wanted to show it to Carrie, that was all.'

Enzo patted her hand. 'It's alright, Millie' he assured her. 'If you had not had done that then Tom might not have sprung into action; he might have just followed you around and then tried to steal your bag when I was not in a position to help you. He needed to retrieve the bottle before you or he left Sicily; his time was running out.' He smiled. 'You provoked him into action and we caught him. Besides, if anyone is to blame, then it's my fault for giving you the bottle in the first place.'

'But my scarf,' she persisted. 'If I had not wrapped the bottle in my scarf then it would not have caught fire.'

To me this did not make much sense and I could see Enzo frowning as he tried to reassure her.

'You could not foresee him smoking a cigarette,' he said. 'You're not responsible for someone's habits. And how were you to know that the material of your scarf was highly flammable?'

'Not the scarf, as such, this,' Millie said, reaching once more into her bag and producing a small bottle containing a thick white lotion. 'This emollient that I use for my psoriasis. I used the scarf to wrap the bottle in, as it leaks. The liquid is highly flammable and there is a warning label on it to keep away from flames, and to be careful that it may contaminate clothing.'

'Even so,' Enzo said, patting her hand again in reassurance, 'you are not to blame; you helped to catch a criminal.'

'That reminds me!' I cried, delving into my bag and retrieving the, by now, creased and slightly crumpled newspaper clipping, 'Tom said that *you* were a criminal! A burglar.' I passed the snippet across.

Enzo glanced at it and smiled. He pointed to the man standing next to him in the picture. 'This man, he's the burglar.' He said. 'I had helped to convict him. This picture was taken after his trial.' I cast my mind back to when I had shown Tom the newspaper. 'I suppose he could have meant the other man.' I was unsure how carefully Tom had looked at the article. 'He might have just made a quick superficial perusal or perhaps his Italian was not as good as he and Angela had maintained.' I added.

'Or he might have just said that to cause a bit of trouble,' Millie suggested. I looked at her to explain. 'If you thought Enzo was a criminal you might not have wanted to encourage his attentions. I don't suppose Tom liked the idea that Enzo was following us, or you around.'

I considered this. 'So he knew you were – are – a policeman?' I asked Enzo.

'Not a policeman, as such,' he explained, 'but an investigator for the Arts and Antiquities Department; but he might not have known that. I just happened to be in that photograph; I'm not mentioned in the accompanying article.'

'So you're the good guy?' I asked.

Enzo nodded. 'I'm the good guy.' He grinned.

'Even though you made out with Vanessa and kissed her in church?'

The smile slipped from his face. 'I needed to keep an eye on your group, and you,' he reminded me with a point of his finger and a very serious expression, 'you, young lady, told me to go away and not to bother you again.'

'Well you have my permission to bother me,' I said. He dipped his head in acknowledge. I thought a moment and then said, 'So what was in the bottle? The thing that Tom picked up and put in his pocket?'

Again, Enzo smiled. 'I was waiting for you to ask that.' He reached into his pocket and took out a tiny marble statue about four inches tall of what appeared to be a blacksmith, his arm raised as he was about to strike down on an anvil, encased in a protective polythene bag. 'He's rather old and rather valuable. Vulcan, the Roman god of fire.'

I've not held a genuine Roman artefact in my hand before, not even one contained within a protective bag. Enzo had first passed it to Millie who considered it before handing it to me. I turned it around. It was exquisite, but I was not sure that it was worth someone's life.

I quickly gave it back to Enzo before I dropped it.

'But the thing I saw Tom pick up was white,' I said. 'It looked like a white blob. This is pale but it's not white; it's variegated with little streaks of colour, pinks and greens.'

Enzo explained that the statue had been encased in bandages with a protective layer of plaster of Paris, the substance used for broken limbs. 'Have you ever noticed in television documentaries archaeologists use a watered down solution of this when excavating fragile objects? It protects them in transit and washes off afterwards.'

He further informed us that he had been investigating a smuggling ring which used bottles of wine to transport small stolen objects.

'At first we thought that they were using the bottles to send coded messages about the thefts until you gave me the idea that the small statues could actually be inside.'

I felt a sudden glow of pleasure that I had helped, but it was short lived. 'Me? I gave you the idea?' So many questions flooded through my brain. 'How do they get the statues inside? I know with a ship in a bottle they insert the boats with the sails and masts lowered and them raise them with removable strings once the vessel is in place, but you could not force a statue through a bottle neck.'

Enzo shook his head. 'Remember the bottle broke into two halves, more or less?' Millie and I nodded in agreement. 'Well, the bottles are cast in two equal pieces and then secured around the statue. All that 'lava' encrusting the outside hides the joins. Also, so as the statues inside are not damaged – notice this statue is not stained or discoloured by red wine? – The outer casings are double.' He noticed our frowns. 'Remember the little girl we saw feeding her doll from a pretend bottle of milk that was actually coloured water?'

I nodded and explained to Millie that she has been at the post office at the time.

'Essentially, those bottles are hollow,' Enzo continues, 'only containing a small amount of liquid between an inner and an outer shell of the bottle, and when tipped up the liquid completes a circuit, giving the impression that the doll has drunk it, before recollecting back in a central reservoir.

'Likewise, these wine bottles are hollow, with just a small amount of fluid, coloured water actually, that moves and gives an appropriate sloshing sound when the bottle is tipped, to give the illusion that it is a full bottle of wine. Also, together with the statue inside and a little protective padding, it is calculated to give the approximate correct weight of a bottle of wine.'

He paused and looked enquiringly at us. Millie and I both dutifully nodded that we understood his explanation. 'Everything was carefully planned, with items stolen to order,' he continued 'Not all the artifacts stolen were marble. It could be a small bronze statuette, for example. The label on the bottle is the exact replica of the model inside, not only a guide so that the thieves can recognise the contents -'

'Tom did ask for a particular bottle at Mount Etna!' I remembered.

'Exactly,' agreed Enzo. 'But also, the statue inside is secured so that it is exactly aligned with the label. We think this was done with the assumption that if a suitcase containing a bottle is put through an X-ray scanning machine at an airport, for example, any image of the statue seen on the scanner screen the thieves hoped it would be assumed to be the picture on the label.' Here, Enzo's eyebrows raised and he gave a little grimace that suggested otherwise.

'But with all the publicity, why did they continue to steal things? It's not as if they can show it to anyone'

Enzo shrugged. 'For some collectors the mere thought that they own something ancient or valuable is sufficient. So what if they cannot, just at the present time, display it; as far as they are concerned it is theirs; ownership is enough.'

The police had eventually allowed our group to leave Vulcano. Once everyone given statements with our home contact details, we were free to travel onto our final hotel for a brief stay. Enzo travelled on the ferry with us and then booked into the same country house hotel on the outskirts of Catania.

We had come a full circle but so much had happened since the last time we had been here. And of course we were a reduced party, without Vanessa or Tom. Angela had been taken to a local hospital suffering from shock. I was concerned about Millie who still seemed very down but was currently keeping Joan company whilst she recuperated with her injured ankle, and both ladies were keeping out of the way of Dottie, who was generally considered to be harmless in the normal scheme of things, until her mania got the better of her.

Which left Enzo and I together in a quiet secluded corner of the lounge bar. I had allowed him to buy me a drink as penance for his past behaviour, which my mother would have called "flighty," and while I casually questioned him about this I also allowed him to sit with his arm around my shoulders, as it felt comfortable.

'So why did you kiss Vanessa in the church?' I asked him.

He swirled the wine in his glass considering his answer. 'You told me to go away,' he said sounding very serious. 'Not to bother you again.' He paused briefly. 'I thought I had made you very angry.' He sipped his wine. 'But I needed to keep an eye on your group as I was sure that someone in the party was the link in the chain, and with Vanessa it was easy, she was so willing, so eager to get acquainted.'

I was reluctant to probe him further on their relationship so instead I asked, 'But what was she doing with Tom? I mean, he was the man I saw climbing over the patio wall in the early hours of the morning, not you, wasn't he?'

Enzo nodded. 'Tom considered himself a lady's man and Vanessa equally thought she was capable of seducing anyone. I admit I planted the suggestion in her mind that he was attracted to her and when I told her I was not following her to Vulcano she transferred her attentions to him.' Enzo took another drink and then continued. 'Which played into my hands, as of course I did follow your group to Vulcano.'

He placed his glass on the table and gently touched my arm. 'I wanted to make sure that you were in no danger, but I also had a job to do. When Tom was in

213

Vanessa's room I entered and stole the bottle; it was quite easy; Angela takes sleeping tablets hence she had no idea Tom had left for the night.'

'And you gave the bottle to Millie for safekeeping,' I said. He nodded ruefully. 'Why didn't you give it to me?' I asked.

'Because I was not sure if you were still angry with me,' he replied. 'Besides, Millie was on the spot so to speak. I mistimed my escape from Angela's room. If was all my own fault,' he gave a typical Italian shrug. 'I had been keeping watch on Vanessa's room, trying to judge how long Tom, he was going to stay there, whether for a short time or to almost spend the night, when I inadvertently dozed off.' Here Enzo dropped his gaze from mine in embarrassment.

'When I awoke, I quickly went to Tom's room for the bottle, but just as I was leaving I spotted him re-entering the hotel, as if he had just been out having a casual early morning stroll around the grounds, if you please. I imagine he stayed with Vanessa until such time that when he went back to his own room, if his wife woke up when he arrived and saw him fully dressed, he could claim he had just got up. Any earlier and she might have been suspicious.

'I bumped into Millie as she was on her way to breakfast. I did not want to be seen with the bottle in my hand so I asked her just to slip it into her bag. Unfortunately, it seems Dottie saw us and was suspicious, hence her attempt to get Millie on her own during your mountain climbing expedition. Millie, on the other hand, asked no questions; she simply agreed to help me out, and to remain silent about seeing me on the island.'

'Hence she lied when she told me she had not seen you,' I said.

Enzo nodded. 'I think having given her the bottle to look after I was on her mind. She was worried, a little anxious, but also she wanted in her own way to reassure you that I was not the person who had spent the night with Vanessa.'

'Which she knew, as you had used that time to break into Tom's room and steal the bottle.' I paused, then added, 'I think Millie is very taken with you.' I twisted my head to look at him; he was smiling.

'Just Millie?' he asked.

I remained silent, I did not want to feed his vanity. Instead I asked him, 'When Tom grabbed Millie and the bottle, why did he not just make a run for it?'

'Ah, that was possibly where I made my mistake in taking the bottle in the first place,' admitted Enzo, 'but I was not sure whether it really was a bottle with a statue inside or a normal bottle like yours, which by the way, was a total accident when I broke it. There was no way that a tourist like yourself would be able to buy one of the special bottles; those were kept to one side until the right person asked for it, and there are actually very few of them about. And also, of course, there had not been enough time from when the statue of Venus was stolen for them to have hidden it inside, even if they had the special bottle in which to hide it already created, and then transport it out to the shop ready to pass onto the buyer.'

Enzo shifted a little uneasily in his seat; suddenly all smiles were gone. 'When Tom noticed the bottle was missing he realised he had been rumbled and organised his escape.'

Enzo paused and I noticed that his eyes looked troubled as he contemplated the consequence of his actions. 'I think he first thought Vanessa had taken it, hence he killed her, expecting her body to be lost at sea, but unluckily for him she caught on the ladder. He arranged for another member of his group to standby with a small boat which was to have sailed up to one of the open sea bathing areas – not the one where Vanessa was found – so he could escape off the island.'

'Leaving Angela behind?'

Enzo nodded. 'Men like Tom are basically very self-centred with a strong survival instinct. I think he did not make an immediate run for it due to arrogance, possibly he planned to calmly light a cigarette and brag that he had won before making his getaway.'

We sat in companionable silence for a while and then I asked 'So I was just a means for you to keep an eye on our group?'

'Of course!' he replied. 'I am a professional; I am very good at my job.'

I poked him in the ribs with my elbow.

'Who would you have suggested I try and seduce?' he asked. 'Joan is so quiet, like a little mouse, Millie is like my mother.'

'Dottie?' I suggested.

216

'Dottie is mad,' he said matter of factly. 'And she is not my type at all.'

'And they're all a bit old for you anyway.'

"Oh, in my line of work, age is no barrier, besides, don't knock experience.'

I nudged him again.

'You are right, of course,' he conceded. 'I knew as soon as I saw you in Taormina that you were the one.'

And having extracted that admission, I let him kiss me.

Yes, I think all things considered, I enjoyed this holiday

Epilogue:

As Enzo had followed us (it had been a little disheartening to discover that primarily he had only been doing his job and not stalking me as a lovesick swain after all) through most of our tour but had not been present at the gorge I asked why, after following us from Taormina to the Greek theatre, he had not trailed us to the Gorge. His answer was simple – his bike had a puncture.

He said it was easy to follow our group as it was an organised tour, which followed the same pattern; once a month a party of tourists arrived, stayed at the same hotels for each visit and followed the same set itinerary.

Dottie had admitted to pushing Joan down the mountainside at Volcano. She had nothing against the other woman other than thinking her rather bland and insipid, but who just happened to be in Dottie's way. She had thought that I would take control of the situation and that she, Dottie, would be left alone with Millie, and she would be able to see if it was something to do with the sword that Millie kept wrapped in her scarf, although, sadly, unaware that usually all Millie had secreted away was her hand lotion and that the bottle Enzo had passed to her was, at that time, locked in her suitcase back at the hotel.

Enzo revealed he had decided I was innocent and he could trust me after he had overheard my comment to Vanessa that the bottle could contain anything when we were at Mount Etna; a person guilty of theft or smuggling would have kept quiet and not drawn attention to the item.

One of Tom's confederates who had been in the boat waiting to help him make his getaway after being apprehended by the coast guards confirmed Enzo's hypothesis regarding the wine bottles. He admitted that the gang had lava used encrusted bottles in an attempt to shield the object during any X-ray process in the same manner that X-ray departments are lead-lined and radiographers wear lead lined aprons to protect themselves, thus they hoped that the volcanic lava possessed similar properties.

They did not consider scanning machines a problem if the object hidden inside the bottle was marble or another similar stone, it was only a concern for a statuette fashioned from metal such as bronze. However, as far as the thieves were concerned airport security is generally on the lookout for explosive liquids or drugs; a bottle of wine in a suitcase stored in the cargo hold, they anticipated, would be unlikely to raise any suspicions.

After our argument Enzo had associated with Vanessa as he needed an excuse to keep an eye on the group; he was adamant that that was the only reason he dallied with her in the cathedral in Syracuse. He furthermore claimed that the time spent with me (and Millie) had been no hardship.

While we waited patiently in the departure area at Catania airport Millie had turned to me and thanked me for looking after her, keeping her company while keeping her out of mischief.

'It was rather fun, wasn't it?' she had said with a little giggle, 'Even if we did not find the sword,' she added a little wistfully. I had to agree, on both counts; most of the time it had been, which made me feel a little guilty as primarily I had sought her company as a means of avoiding spending time with Vanessa and fanning that woman's vanity as she held court to relate her (in her own opinion) glamorous lifestyle whilst sipping endless glasses of white wine. Then I felt guilty for thinking ill of the dead.

The rest of the tourists in our group, as far as I know, turned out to be exactly who they claimed to be, and perfectly harmless individuals for the most part (although I think the jury is still out on Dottie).

Pat's bottle only contained red wine; there was no extra gift of a tiny statue of Venus such as you might find in a cereal packet, not even one made of plastic.

As far as I am aware, to date Excalibur has not been found in Sicily, or anywhere else for that matter.

If you enjoyed reading *Playing With Fire*, please consider leaving a review online.

You might also like to subscribe to my mailing list using this online link: http://eepurl.com/ilO-Z2 for updates on new releases etc, and receive a free story as a thank you. Please allow 24 hours for the story to come through.

Carrie and Keith Mysteries:

1. Material Witness. Summer 2012.

A light hearted cozy style suspense/ghost story, set in Dorset on the English south coast during the summer of 2012.

Carrie discovers internet shopping, and soon develops an addiction for vintage clothes. Her interest is piqued by a Victorian mourning cloak and deciding to delve into the background of its former owner, she adds a wedding dress to her collection. After discovering the promised photograph of the original bride is missing from the parcel she feels cheated and sets out to track down what she sees as her property.

Meanwhile she is also agonizing over her one-sided relationship with Keith, a man with a young nephew, whom she met on the bus.

But *is* Colin really Keith's nephew? And have her actions put him in danger?

Who broke into her garage and why?

And why, at odd moments, can she smell lavender?

It seems that one of Carrie's purchases has brought with it a little unforeseen *something* extra that sends her off onto a new obsessive tangent, and a journey into the past, as she determines to uncover the truth.

The first in a series that can also be read as a standalone novel.

2. Thirteen in the Medina. Autumn 2012.

Following the stresses of the summer Carrie prepares to go on holiday only to find Keith (who has had a haircut but grown a rather long beard instead) tagging along after securing a cancellation in an effort to avoid babysitting Colin.

However, thirteen is unlucky for some and if Carrie is hoping for a holiday romance she is doomed for disappointment as Keith falls into the clutches of an older woman (but she only has herself to blame after urging him to mingle). Carrie worries that her friend may be being used as a drugs' mule only to become aware that she is the person who may be in danger.

Following several strange occurrences Carrie is left pondering just how many pairs of (brightly coloured) shorts has Keith packed and why is there a man in black lurking by the swimming pool?

Another slow burning story set against the backdrop of a North African sun, as Carrie tours Morocco whilst her changing relationship with Keith mirrors the twists and turns of the medina, as it gently, and humorously, moves towards its climax as the end of their vacation nears.

Carrie and Keith Short Stories:

Seasonal Shorts

Seven spine tingling tales of the paranormal told with a light hearted touch, including the previously published "The Way to Nowhere" and "All at Sea."

When Keith suggests a trip to Tunisia staying in separate rooms Carrie decides to eye up the other men on the tour: is their relationship coming to an end, or is there a malignant presence influencing her actions?

And the last thought that went swirling around my brain as I fell asleep was that something was wrong if I no longer fancied Keith; I obviously was not myself. **At the Edge**

Carrie's attempt to knit Keith a sweater for Christmas using second-hand wool turns into a disaster.

'A jumper down to your knees is called a dress,' Pat informed me. 'Nothing wrong with a woollen dress.'
Woolly Woes

'So, where does the path lead?' I asked him.
'To the aviary.'
'But there is no aviary; the aviary does not exist,' I protested.
'So, where does the path lead? **The way to Nowhere**

They meet a distressed man undertaking a futile search for a lost dog, or is he engaged in a more tragic quest?

'It isn't just soldiers who die in wartime.' **Desperately Seeking Freddie**

In these troubled times it is considered wrong to express too much interest in other people's children - should I have taken more notice of the activities of someone else's child for whom I was not responsible, in order to ensure his safety, if he appeared to be alone? **All at Sea**

After Katie is stood up by her date she faces a nervous walk late at night.

She still felt a prickle down her spine. **He's Behind You**

Pat is annoyed by a persistent carol singer whilst housesitting for an elderly aunt just before Christmas.

'If he does requests,' Pat hissed in my ear, 'ask him to go away.' **The Voice of an Angel**

Digital Short Stories:

The Way to Nowhere

When Keith volunteers to hand deliver an urgent letter to the Civic Centre Carrie agrees to accompany him. A serious road accident in the vicinity results in them taking a short cut through Poole Park at dusk where they see an unusually dressed woman waiting by a signpost pointing towards an aviary, and Carrie loses her bracelet.

The following day Carrie tries to retrace her steps in order to find the bracelet but cannot locate either the path they followed nor find any trace of an aviary.

She enlists Keith's help and whilst searching they come across Frankie, a small boy who has had an accident on his scooter, and who has an intriguing reason for his mishap.

Along with Pat, whose grandfather, a former park keeper who had maintained the park was haunted, they decide to research into its history trying to find evidence for the apocryphal aviary.

Can Carrie and Keith find the path again?

And if they do, what will they discover if they try to follow it to its end? Does it lead to an aviary, or to somewhere more dangerous?

All at Sea

Carrie is hoping for a quiet, relaxing day at the beach with Keith and Colin, however two uninvited children seem to have other ideas, leaving her struggling with a moral dilemma.

A short ghost story set at the seaside.

Printed in Great Britain
by Amazon